TRAIN✦FLIGHT

THE SANCTUARY

ELIZABETH NEWTON

Imprint: Salt and Light Press

SALT & LIGHT
— PRESS —

All Rights Reserved
First Edition

Newton, Elizabeth (author)
Train Flight
Book 3: The Sanctuary
ISBN 978-1-7640008-2-6

For J.

BOOK THREE

This story is the third of the Train Flight series. It can be read by itself, but it is also part of the ongoing adventures of Evie and Paulo on the Train with the Captain.

Others in the series so far:
1. Moon Man
2. The Birth of Salvation

The Engine Room

TRAIN RULES:

1. Stay with Captain
2. Don't wander off
3. Let Captain do the talking
4. Don't ask too many unnecessary questions
5. Always make sure your shoelaces are tied up tight.

CHAPTER

1

FORGETTING

The thing about holidays is that everybody has a different idea about what the perfect holiday is like. Some people think holidays should be filled with activity. Jet-skiing, skydiving, mountain-climbing, zero-gravity golf, shark-surfing, or as much of all-of-the-above as possible. For other people, this would be a complete nightmare. These people prefer a quiet log cabin in a forest somewhere with nothing to do but read books and sip hot chocolate by a fireplace.

Some love meeting new people and learning new things. Some want to get as far away from other people as possible and forget everything they've ever learned for a month.

Whatever your ideal holiday, *the Sanctuary* has something for you. Your perfect home away from home crafted to suit your tastes and personality. Every moment, every detail extracted directly from your memories, your dreams, your longings. And you never have to leave!

Are you ready for that perfect retreat? Your perfect escape? Your *Sanctury*...

"Next patient please," said a tall, young woman with a clipboard. She emerged stiffly from a dimly lit consulting room, wearing glasses, a modest blouse, and grey pencil skirt. Her dull brown hair was in a loose, sensible bun.

Leela Patson awkwardly stood up and followed the consultant into the room. When the consultant sat down behind her desk, she heard a voice in her head: *Remember, it is important not to refer to them as patients. They are* **clients**. She flashed a smile. "My name's Sue. Now, why don't you tell me what's on your mind?"

"Well, I'm just so stressed right now. They've given me extra assignments at school because they think I need more challenges. My parents expect me to do it all on top of my music lessons and team captain responsibilities but they're never around because of *their* extra work hours. So I have to look after my siblings and sometimes cook the meals too. My youngest sister has to have all these tests done and maybe go to a special school, which is going to cost a lot so now Dad reckons I should get a job too to help pay for everything. I want to go on this music camp but my parents will say it's too expensive and they need me here..."

Sue was nodding sympathetically.

"I don't know if this amount of stuff's normal for a high-school kid..." Leela pushed a strand of hair behind her ear with a clammy, shaking hand. "...and I just can't see an out. I can't see when it's ever going to get any easier..."

Sue walked around to the front of her desk. She spoke in a calm, breathy voice as though she was trying to calm a spooked horse. "I understand. It is very *stressful,* isn't it?"

"Sometimes I wish I could just... stop. Even for a day or a week or something."

"You want to escape. Forget it all."

3

"If only. But I know can't let my family down. I just came here so that I could have a good chat about it. I can't talk to anyone else."

"Let your stress go, right now in this room."

Leela closed her eyes and exhaled a long, slow breath.

"Imagine... it *is* possible. You have no responsibilities. Nothing to do. Your family is far away. In fact, perhaps, just for a moment, you *have* no family. No one is relying on you."

Leela sighed and smiled. "That sounds good. Thing is, all my problems are back as soon as I go back home to my family."

"You *have* no family. Remember?" The consultant smiled. Then she said in her gentle, whispery voice, "Come through."

Leela opened her eyes. "Through to where?"

"Another room. It's called the forgetting room."

Odd, thought Leela. *Must be part of the therapy.* She followed the consultant through another doorway.

Once they were inside, the calm, sympathetic consultant quietly closed the door behind them.

And that's when the blinding light and the terrible screeching happened. That was the moment when Leela Patson... escaped it all.

If you're a time traveller, you'll know that time is relative. This means that it behaves differently or passes at a different rate depending on where and when you are. So, at about this same time, relatively speaking, the Captain of the Train♣ and one of his passengers, Paulo,♦ were standing on a vast, beautiful, open, green hilltop. The sky was bright and gleaming blue, with radiant sunlight glistening off each blade of lush grass. The fresh, clean smell of nature filled their noses, and the sweet sound of bird song and gentle breezes graced their ears.

Evie Bamford, another of the Train's passengers, was wandering off, soaking it all up.♠ She seemed not to care that they had no idea where they were, that something had gone wrong with the controls of the Train, and that the Captain and Paulo were calling to her at the top of their lungs.

♣ **Train** /treɪn/: [1] *n.* a set of carriages or wagons, whether self-propelled or connected to a locomotive. [2] *v.* to discipline and instruct a person or animal to perform specified actions. [3] *n.* a vehicle made from the wreckage of a railway steam train that travels in space and time, the paint work of which enabling it to 'appear' invisible.

♦ Paulo was a boy from a planet called Serothia, found in the Black Eye galaxy (or M64), seventeen million lightyears away from Earth.

♠ Evie Bamford was from South Australia, on Earth. She was thirteen and her bursting curiosity had landed her on the Train not long ago.

"If we're not on your planet Captain," said Paulo, "where are we exactly?"

"Well I hate to worry you," replied the Captain in his distinguished, English, everything-under-control tone, "but I have no idea. Usually when I land on a new planet, I could give you a rough idea of at least what galaxy we're in. But the Train seems to be confused about this place; it won't give me a reading. We *were* meant to have landed on my home world but..."

"It's beautiful here."

"Exactly. Definitely can't be my home."

"It could very well be Serothia," said Paulo.

"It could very well be Evelyn's Earth too," said the Captain. "It could very well be any number of different planets. Come on, let's see if we can get the Train back on track. It's time I got Evelyn home." On his way to the Train door, the Captain called out again, "Evelyn! All aboard!"

"What's she doing?" said Paulo softly.

Evie was walking down the hill, taking slow, even steps. She was holding a delicate white flower against her chest that she'd picked from the ground. *It's so beautiful here,* she was thinking. *I think I want to stay here forever. So peaceful. Quiet. Tranquil. Peaceful...*

"Evelyn!" the Captain called loudly.

She was close enough to hear him, but she kept on walking, like she was in some kind of trance.

"I'll go get her," said Paulo and took off with a jog down the hill.

But the Captain suddenly yelled to stop him. "No, stop Paulo! Get away!"

Paulo's eyes widened with terrified alarm. They both saw a strange glow, brightening all around Evie's body. Then an ear-piercing screeching sound screamed across the hills.

What a perfect place. The air is so fresh. The ground is so soft. I want to live here...

Both the Captain and Paulo were shielding their ears and eyes, but after a moment, the sound stopped. They looked up. The light, the sound, everything was gone. Evelyn was gone. If they didn't know any better, it would have seemed like that beautiful clear countryside had no memory of her ever having been there.

CHAPTER

THE RECOVERY ROOM

Paulo scrambled to his feet, looking all around. "What happened?"

The Captain scratched his head. "Transmat beam, teleportation, hole in the ground... could be any number of things."

"But can I just check with you... that I'm not seeing things. She *has* actually completely *vanished?*"

"Well, we can't be too sure of that either. She could be there, and we just can't see her."

"But she disappeared right before our eyes."

"Not right before our eyes. The light was so bright we couldn't see anything, could we."

"That's true. Anything could have happened."

They made their way down the hill a little, looking up, down, and all around.

"Can't have been a transmat beam," Paulo said.

"Why do you say that?"

"Well there's usually a peculiar sort of *buzz* in the air when there's just been a matter transfer."

"The residual energy lingering from dispersed atoms."

Paulo nodded. "Well I can't sense it here."♣

"Good observation, Paulo. So if it wasn't matter transfer..." the Captain jumped up and down, "ground seems firm..."

"What else is there?"

"Either somebody just rushed over to her and grabbed her while we weren't looking... or something much more clever and sinister is going on."

"There's nothing out here to hide behind. Not for miles anyway."

"Evelyn!!" called the Captain, with his hands cupped around his mouth. "She seemed... odd before she disappeared don't you think?"

"Yes she did. She wasn't paying any attention to us; she just wandered off. And it was like she

---

♣ They had been using matter transfer technology for a good many years on Serothia.

couldn't even hear that screechy sound."

"And she knows not to wander off."

"Perhaps we should 'wander off' too, see if anything happens."

"Sounds highly risky Paulo. I like it. Come on."

For a few seconds, Evie couldn't open her eyes. They felt glued together with gunky sleep. When she did eventually get them open, all she could see was a high blurry ceiling, way up above her. A harsh, white, buzzing light was glaring down at her. She blinked a few times to get her vision into focus. She tried to sit up but her head started swimming, she had to pause. She blinked, rubbed her head, and it was a full minute before she could properly sit upright. She was in a white hospital bed, with white sheets and a white blanket. Her bed was one of many, all lined up along the walls, parallel with each other. They were all empty except for hers.

There were large square windows spread evenly along one wall. At least, Evie assumed they were windows; they were all hidden behind thick curtains. They were dark orange with bright yellow flowers all over them, as if someone had attempted to brighten up the room with them, and failed dismally.

Evie lifted the bed covers off and swung her legs around to place her feet on the floor. And there she stayed for another few minutes, waiting for her head to clear. She was trying to remember how she got here. She had been with the Captain and Paulo on this beautiful lush green hillside...

This isn't the right place, the Captain had said.

Of course it's the right place, Evie had replied. *It's perfect!*

That's the last thing I remember, she frowned.

She stood up slowly from the bed and stepped around silently, looking for any sign of life. It was a dated looking hospital ward. *Perhaps I'm in the 1940s,* she thought. Now that she'd met the Captain, anything was possible. For some reason the empty beds were creepy. *Maybe it's an abandoned 1940s hospital...*

"Up and about I see?" a voice echoed.

Evie jumped around and saw a young woman in an old-school white nurse's outfit.

Evie just had to ask the inevitable question. She did it very politely. "W-where am I, please?"

"In the Infirmary."

"What's an infirmary?"

The nurse was taken aback for a moment. "The rest bay... the hospice."

"As in, hospital?"

The nurse gave a polite smile. "The word 'hospital' has stigma, we feel."

"What's stigma?"

"I think you ought to be getting back to bed, D14. You may need some more rest before we release you. It's important you understand that there's no hurry to recover. You can take as long as you need."

The nurse tried to hustle her back into bed, but Evie protested. "Recover from what, and... what did you call me?"

"In you get, there's a good girl."

Evie stood her ground. "I feel fine! I don't need any more rest. Tell me where I am, please."

"I told you. The Infirmary."

"But *where*. The Infirmary of *where*?"

"Surely you know where you are. You're in the

12

Sanctuary, my dear."

Evie frowned deeper. The calmness of the nurse was making her nervous. Which, I'm quite sure, is the opposite effect that a calm voice usually goes for.

A new voice then boomed. "Alright, sister. It's alright, I'll deal with this one." Evie looked to the door again. There was another woman in a nurse's uniform, walking briskly towards them. This one was older, bigger, matronly. She didn't look quite as calm as the younger nurse, who now gave the older one a little nod and then left the room.

The head-nurse, or matron, or whatever she was, spoke to Evie with a stern manner. "You'll have to excuse 81Z3, she didn't realise you're new here."

"Did you say *eighty-one zed three*?"

"Now that you're out of bed and feeling up to things, you'd better follow me to the Recovery Room." She started walking, expecting Evelyn to follow her.

Well, the woman was her only hope of answers, so Evie did follow. And after a short walk down a very drab and musty hallway with more of the orange and yellow curtains, they came to a door. The matron opened it and led Evie through.

The room beyond was very different from the hallway. The bright, natural sunlight coming

13

through the many large windows was lovely, but the rest of the room gave Evie a strange unease. It felt like the voice of the nurse earlier. Calmness being forced upon her.

The furniture had no sharp corners or edges, just smooth, curvy, slopey lines. There was nauseating music playing, like someone was attempting to play classical music with things other than musical instruments. The occupants of the room, however, seemed perfectly content with it. Not that they gave much clue about how they felt; the fourteen or fifteen of them, spanning all ages, were behaving just as peculiarly. Some of them, grown men and women, were playing with toddler toys. The kind you might find in a doctor's waiting room. Some of them were just staring out the window, and others were gazing at simple paintings on the wall. Two or three of them were doing nothing but sitting in a chair, staring blankly at the air in front of them.

"You'll be quite comfortable here, while you recover from your rest," said the matron.

That's funny, Evie thought. *I was just thinking how uncomfortable I was feeling.*

Before Evie could stop her, the matron closed her in there. Evie grabbed the handle and jiggled, but it was locked. None of the other occupants paid any attention. One girl, who looked only a little older than herself, sitting by a window, did give her a tiny smile, so Evie walked over to her.

"Hello," she said softly.

The girl just smiled, and as Evie knelt in front of her chair, she realised the girl wasn't looking directly back into her eyes. It was like she was looking straight through her. Evie waved a hand in front of her face. There was no response. Just her calm, empty smile.

"How long have we been walking now?" called Paulo, dragging his feet.

The Captain grabbed his fob watch which hung by a chain from a pocket in his knitted waistcoat. "Almost thirty minutes."

"Feels longer. Like we've been wandering around for nearly half an hour!"

"Half an hour *is* thirty..."

"Can we rest under those trees over here?"

"Alright, for a short while."

The Captain joined Paulo in the shade of a dozen or so trees. Paulo could see that the Captain was thinking very hard about something.

"What are you thinking?"

"Only how much I wish I still had my other Unique Radio-Wave-Operated Link-Chip. And that Evelyn had it with her. Then we could track her."

"But even if it didn't just get destroyed in ancient Jerusalem, it wouldn't be in Evie's possession."

"I know. Just shows how being tired can cause one to think irrationally."

"You know, when I met you, I didn't think it was possible for you to get tired."

"Oh it is, Paulo. I'm just as human as you are. But perhaps this planet's mass is greater than what we're used to. It would make the force of gravity stronger, weighing us down."

Paulo inclined his head to one side. "I don't actually know where you *are* from, Captain. I mean, are you from Earth like Evelyn? Or from yet another planet I haven't heard of. I know you're not from my planet."

"It's a little complicated," the Captain said, gloomily. "My home is..."

"Aaahhhhhhh!" came the angry cry of many voices. A group of men and women were suddenly charging at them from all sides holding sticks and stones. Within seconds, Paulo and the Captain were surrounded. The attackers were well-tanned and wore tattered street clothes. Some had a collection of scratches and bruises. One of them, a tall, lean man, raised an arm and the mob stopped shouting. Without taking his eyes off the two stunned travellers, he inched toward them, step by step, maintaining a combat stance.

"Afternoon," the Captain said with a friendly smile. "Lovely day."

"Grab them!" yelled the leader, and they all lunged forward to restrain their arms with animal-like aggression. These ruffians were predators, and the Captain and Paulo appeared to be their prey.

CHAPTER

SANCTUARY

||||||||||||||||||||||||||||||||||||||||||||||||||

"Next client please?"

A young man with a red, blotchy face and bloodshot eyes walked slowly into a consulting room as though his feet were sinking into quicksand with every step.

Another man, this one wearing a suit and tie, welcomed him to a seat. "Don't be afraid," he said calmly. "My name's Mark. "Now, what's troubling you?"

"Well," said the young man, quietly, "I've been living with my brother and now he's kicked me out."

"I see. Is this for a short while? He's trying to teach you a lesson? That sort of thing?"

"No. This is for good. He doesn't want a bar of

me. I've been in a dark place lately, but he thinks I'm just lazy. What should I do?"

"I can't get your brother to let you move back in, I'm afraid. But I know exactly what you need."

"What's that?" the young man sniffed.

The suited man smiled tenderly, stood up and led his client to an adjoining room. "Come this way."

The lad got up and followed the consultant.

In another room, a long way away, on another planet as a matter of fact, another man, sitting at a desk, was watching the whole situation going on right in front of him on a huge wide screen. "Yes," he was saying, "that's right. That's right. He *needs* us, the poor chap. He needs the Forgetting Room."

Mark quietly closed the door. The Forgetting Room was sound-proofed of course. The screeching could never be heard from the waiting rooms.

Evie would have gone mad if she hadn't decided to recite the first ten elements of the periodic table over and over again in her head. Sitting in this room, with these mad people, listening to this mad music, for a maddening amount of time... it was surely the periodic table that saved her. She wondered why it was that she was the only person in the room noticing how weird it all was. Everyone else seemed to be a part of it.

Someone finally came back into the room. This time, it was a man with a white t-shirt and white trousers. He had called "D14" as soon as he entered but got no response. So he came all the way into the room where Evie was, looked straight into her eyes and again called, "D14!"

Then Evie remembered, *she* was D14. Apparently. She stood up, looking at the nurse. The kind-faced man nodded and raised his arm, signalling towards the door.

"Why don't you just call me Evie, it's not that difficult to say, is it?"

The nurse didn't reply. He led her through several more musty hallways, and then finally, out of the building.

The open air! Evie breathed in a long, deep lung-full of it. But she couldn't enjoy it for long; only seconds later, it was straight back inside, into the back seat of an old-fashioned car painted pink and pale green. Before she managed to get a look at the driver, the car took off along a winding road.

"Excuse me," Evie said, bravely, "where am I being taken to?"

"Home of course, D14," was the reply.

She frowned, utterly confused. "...Home?"

"What's the meaning of this?" the Captain said to the angry mob. "We haven't done anything to you. I can't imagine why you're attacking us. Unless of course we're your dinner." He erupted into laughter as he said it, but the capturers were not even smiling.

The Captain cleared his throat after a brief glance at Paulo. "We're... not your... dinner... are we?"

"Stop it, Captain," whispered Paulo. "You're giving them ideas."

"Calm yourself," the leader suddenly said, lowering his spear. "We're not going to eat you."

The two breathed a sigh of relief.

"We must always detain any wanderers, to

evaluate their intentions. What *are* your intentions?"

"Well..." said the Captain, "our intentions are to find a lost friend of ours. Something went wrong with our coordinates and... well, we took a wrong turn as they say."

"You're here by *accident?*"

"Yes we are," said Paulo.

"You have your own craft?"

Paulo was about to answer but the Captain stopped him. "Er... we were brought here... by a person who was flying a craft of some sort."♣

"Why do you need to know?" asked Paulo.

Instead of answering, the leader called out to the rest of his group. "Lay down your weapons. We will assist these unfortunate travellers." Then he made proper eye contact with them and this time, his eyes were friendly. "My name is Asher, and I think we may be able to help you."

"That's very decent of you. I'm the Captain, and this is my friend Paulo. And to be honest with you, some help would definitely be very welcome at the moment. May I ask... who are you people, and what are you doing out here?"

♣ Due to past experience, the Captain was careful about what he gave away. Last time someone discovered he had a spaceship, it was stolen.

Asher and his group had a bit of a tribal look about them. Some of their clothes had been patched up and altered with materials from the environment. Leaves, feathers, skins...

"We're... *existing*," replied Asher. "There's not much on this planet outside the Sanctuary."

"What's the Sanctuary?" asked the Captain.

"The Sanctuary?" Asher frowned. "It's the purpose of this planet. The only reason you'd come here is if you're destined for the Sanctuary."

"But what is it?" said Paulo. "*Where* is it? Maybe Evie's there."

"I have no doubt your friend's there," said Asher. "No one lasts long out here on their own."

The Captain looked around. "This doesn't look like a harsh environment. There'd be plenty of resources and agreeable weather to survive on."

"It's not about survival," said Asher. "It's about staying free."

The Captain looked back at Asher for a moment. "Free? Tell me about this place, this er... *Sanctuary*."

"We all came from the Sanctuary," said Asher.

"Not originally, you understand," said another. "We all just lived there for a time."

"At different times," said Asher. "And at different times, we all got away, met up on the outside and now we're out here, trying to live off the earth."

"This planet isn't actually called *Earth* though, is it?" said the Captain.

"We wouldn't have a clue what this planet is called. We're not here by choice. I'm from a planet called Zoran. Elka here is from Maltor, Jon and Pintz, they're both from Sharr Three..."

"Those worlds all have hundreds of light-years between them!" said the Captain, stunned.

"You know them then?"

"I've heard of them, yes. Their positions in the cosmos are very widespread. How did you come to be here in one place?"

"We were all brought here," said Elka.

"To the Sanctuary," Jon clarified.

"By whom?"

"By someone very powerful," Asher said darkly.

"And what do you mean you 'got away' earlier?" the Captain asked. "Do you mean you escaped?"

"Of course. You have to escape. They don't let you walk out."

"What kind of a place *is* this?" asked Paulo.

"Haven't you got the gist yet? It's like a prison. And they always come looking for what gets out."

CHAPTER

HOME SWEET HOME

Despite her first impressions, Evie caught herself thinking what a charming place this was. As the pink and green car took her quietly through narrow, winding, cobblestone lanes, she smiled, imagining she was in some quaint, historical, Northern European country village. There were stone-walled, ivy-covered cottages, local village shops, and old-fashioned streetlamps. Trees lined the sides of the roads casting picturesque, dappled shadows across the cobblestone, and there was a fresh mild breeze moving playfully through the air.

Her confusion and uncertainty unfortunately overshadowed the experience though. As beautiful as it was, it was still a mystery why she was here.

Everything strange and different... until the car veered slowly around the last corner of the trip and suddenly, she saw her house. Yes, as in, her *actual* house. Home to the Bamford family in Adelaide, Australia, Earth! Evie's mouth dropped open as she stared out the window at it. "I really *am* home," she heard herself say.

"Of course, D14," said the driver.

Everything was just the way it was when she last saw it. The half-finished paint job on the front fence, the petunias she helped her mum plant last week, the silky oak leaves lying all over the front lawn that Dad had been meaning to rake up. But the neighbours' houses were different, and in place of the number 27 on the letterbox, it said 'D14'.

Evie slowly got out of the car and while she was still staring at the house, the car drove off, leaving her alone in the street. She looked all around in amazement. It was as if some big claw on a crane had picked up her home from Adelaide – garden and all – and plonked it down here. She walked cautiously up the path to the front door. The lights were on inside, but all was quiet. The door wasn't locked... and seeing her house again after travelling on the Train was strange.

Home has a way of resetting you. When you're there, it almost feels like the world outside doesn't

26

exist, or that it's in another dimension. For Evie it felt like none of the last few days had even happened. But she had to remind herself that it was all still happening. This was still the world outside. It had to be. ...Or was it?

"Mum? Dad?" she called out. Then she called up the hallway towards her brother's room. "James?" She ran through the kitchen and out to the backyard. "Is anybody here? Hello!?"

She came back inside, into the silence. Every corner, every half-finished task, the few dirty dishes on the sink, the crooked cushions on the couch, were all silent. A shiver ran down her spine.

She eyed her favourite chair in the loungeroom and flopped down into it. The natural thing then was to grab the T.V. remote control and turn the T.V. on. After a bit of flicking around, she realised there were no recognisable channels, it was all different. And all boring. The most boring one was a man talking. He was sitting in a sleek, black swivel chair, talking to the camera. His head was balding and his most noticeable feature was his large nose with a rosy, bulbous tip. The fact that the man's nose and balding head were the only thing she remembered from the five seconds she watched of it, can give you an idea of how boring it was.

She switched it off and got up. It was the same

kind of chair physically, but it didn't feel completely right somehow. Like it was just a copy of the one in her real house.

This whole place is a copy, isn't it? she thought. *It must be.* She went up the hall and entered her own bedroom. How nice it was to see it again. Everything was as it was when she'd left it – to the last detail. From the ball of blue-coloured tack she had stuck on the wall next to her ultra-messy desk, to the three pairs of socks on the floor that she hadn't put in the wash basket yet.

She went to her desk and picked up her diary. She thought she might carry it around with her and write about all her recent adventures. But when she opened it up, she found there was nothing written in it so far. She knew she'd already filled up nearly half of it, but this one was empty, even though the cover was exactly the same. She opened the top drawer to get a pen but there was nothing in the drawer. Usually she'd have trouble even opening it because of all the things she'd stuffed in there... but all the drawers were empty.

So she then ran around the whole house, opening drawers and cupboards and boxes and wardrobes. All of them empty! Under the beds were vacant and bottom sheets were plain white when she knew her own were pale blue with white stars on it. Book covers were all complete and detailed but inside them were blank. The kitchen cupboards and drawers were empty and the fridge too, was empty. (Even though all the correct photographs and magnets were stuck on the front.)

It was then that Evie knew. It was all for show. Nothing was real. It was like a photograph. The only details you're given are what you can see, without moving or opening anything.

While gazing around the kitchen, she suddenly noticed something that wasn't an original item in her own house – something out of place. It was a leaflet on the kitchen cupboard-top, next to the

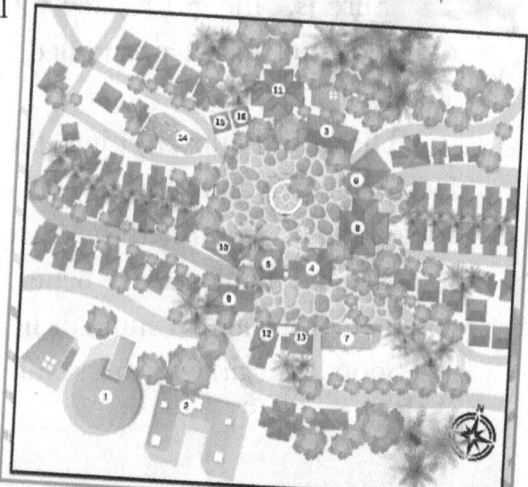

1. Administration Building
2. Infirmary
3. The Sanctuary Convenience Store
4. The Sanctuary Café
5. The Sanctuary Chemist
6. The Sanctuary Hair Salon
7. The Sanctuary Cinema
8. The Sanctuary Art Gallery
9. Sanctuary Spa
10. Sanctuary Clothing and Gifts
11. The Sanctuary Museum
12. All-cultures cuisine
13. Sanctuary Books
14. The Sanctuary Post Office
15. Jewellery Boutique
16. Sanctuary Paper Shop

tea and coffee canisters. She picked it up. On the front, it said *The Sanctuary Square,* and in it were listed all sorts of different shops and facilities and their location on a map. Evie put it inside her pocket and decided to leave the house. It was too quiet and too weird, she'd had enough of it for the time being. Time to look for the *Sanctuary Square.*

She reckoned she'd seen a glimpse of it from the car and it wasn't all that far to walk back. She couldn't help but smile again as she approached. It was a quaint country village square, like something out of the movies. Creeping ivy clung to the old stone buildings, little pots of flowers were growing outside shop fronts, and an attractive fountain stood in the middle of the square. She spotted a café with dainty tables and chairs outside. She walked up to a girl who was clearing away a cup and a plate from one of the tables. "Is this the Sanctuary Café?"

"Sure is," the girl replied with a smile. "Why don't you pull up a chair and sit down? I'll bring you a menu."

The girl disappeared into the café, so Evie, a little cautious and unsure, sat down. It was a gorgeous day, she wished she could enjoy it with the Captain and Paulo. Even better, she wished she could enjoy it with her mum or her school friends!

Soon, the girl was back with a menu. It all

looked very simple; tea, coffee, milkshakes, juices, toasted sandwiches, cakes. She looked up from the menu and saw a lady at another table opposite, also looking over the menu. Evie decided to be brave and go and talk to her.

"I'm new here," Evie said, "what's the nicest thing to eat?"

"The tuna and salad baguette I think. It's what I always get," the woman said kindly.

"I don't like tuna much."

"Well you'd better not get it then. Perhaps the chicken one."

"How long have you been here?"

"Oh, um... it would be about er... ha, do you know something, I can't remember. That's how wonderful this place is. Makes you forget all your troubles."

"Do you like it here?"

"Like it? Of course I do. It's so peaceful and relaxing. Don't you agree?"

"...Yes, it's peaceful and relaxing alright. I just don't know how I got here."

"Oh don't worry about that. Just think about how care-free your life will be now that you *are* here."

"What were you doing before you came here?"

"Oh I was... some sort of instructor. I taught

31

little people all sorts of things – spelling, grammar, science and, what is it they call... er... ma... math... mathematics, that's the word."

"You were a schoolteacher?"

"Yes, that sounds about right. So stressful at times! Busy busy busy, all the time, not a moment to myself. I knew I had to do something about it."

"And... now you're here."

"Exactly. Well, I seem to remember I went to see a... thera... oh what was she called?"

"How long for?"

"What do you mean?"

"Well... how long's your holiday going to be?"

"Oh, you misunderstand. No, I *live* here. *Therapist.* That's the word. I saw a therapist. Before coming here."

"And... what do you do here?"

"What do you mean, what do I *do* here?"

"What do you do for a job, for a living? Are you still teaching?"

"Teaching? Are you joking? I do nothing. I'm a lady of leisure. Have been for years and years and years."

Evie looked at her, thinking she didn't look old enough to have been a teacher and then stopped years and years and years ago.

The waitress of the café came over to the table.

"Have you decided?"

"I don't have any money," replied Evie.

"Money? Just tell me your name dear."

"Evie."

"No... that can't be right..."

"Oh, um... D14? ...I think."

"What would you like, D14?"

"Chicken and salad baguette? And... may I have an orange juice too?"

"And I'll have the tuna thanks F67, same as always," said the other lady.

"Fine. Won't be long." The waitress smiled and walked briskly off with their orders written down on a pad.

"So you're D14," said the woman. "It's nice to meet your acquaintance. I'm 81C3."

Evie repeated slowly, "Eighty-one ...C three."

"Yes, the Sanctuary is wonderful," 81C3 sighed, looking up to the sky and soaking up the sunlight. "I'd almost completely forgotten all that teacher and therapist business before you mentioned it."

Evie was still frowning. She guessed that 81C3 had perhaps almost completely forgotten her whole life as well.

Soon after they finished their baguettes, 81C3 left, and Evie glanced around the café again – at all the people sitting on the outside tables and then all the people sitting at tables inside the building. They all had that same relaxed, burden-free look on their faces as the woman did. But apart from her own conversation with 81C3, not many people talked to one another. There wasn't the constant hum of chit chat like you'd normally hear when you're out and about in public. Although they all seemed happy, it gave Evie that uneasy feeling again.

She turned back around to her own little table to finish the last sip of her orange juice and jumped with fright. There was now a man sitting opposite her where 81C3 had been.

"Good afternoon, D14. It's a pleasure to finally welcome you personally to your new home."

Evie soon recognised him as the man she'd seen on the T.V. The one with the balding head and big nose. He spoke with a deep, commanding voice with a pleasant, posh English accent, and a pleasant, friendly smile. Everything about him was pleasant. Only, perhaps too pleasant.

"Who are you?"

"I am called A1. I trust you've settled in well, and that your home is comfortable."

"It's not my home."

A1 inclined his head to one side and simply said, "Mmm. Interesting."

"Well it looks like it. But it's not."

34

"Very interesting."

"Why am I here?" she asked timidly. "And how did you know what my house looks like?"

"Oh it was nothing," he said calmly, with a modest smile, "you can thank me later. All I wanted to do for the time being was welcome you and let you know that all of this..." he signalled the café, the shops, the gardens, and all around, "is yours. It's your home now. Enjoy it."

"But..."

"When I say *yours*, I mean it's still a public place, so you can't go round doing just anything you please." He laughed, but Evie didn't. "Just, make yourself at home. Make some friends. And if there's anything you need, just drop a little note in the suggestion box in the square, okay."

Evie turned and looked around the square again. "But, what is this place and how did I get here?" But when she looked back... A1 was gone.

It didn't take long for Evie to get fed up with the people in the square and their silly little contented empty smiles. She had to get away. And not back to her house either. That was just as bad. She decided to try and find her way out. Or at least, away from the houses and streets and perfect little fountains. She followed a lane that wound up a hill and out of the village. Then as she came upon an open grassy

35

hillside, she was again reminded of those moments before she'd woken in the hospital bed.

Maybe this is the way I came in.

Logical enough conclusion I suppose.

Which means it could also be the way out!

Well...

It must be. If they haven't done anything silly and wandered off, the Captain and Paulo should be out there somewhere looking for me.

Well let's say, they are looking...

Evie looked behind her.

I'm just going to run for it.

It was looking promising. Nothing but green grass ahead of her; just like what they saw when the Train arrived. But when she was a few metres out, something strange happened. She felt a gentle nudging behind her left shoulder, and when she walked a few more steps, intending to go straight forward, it seemed that she was turning around to the right. When she looked up again, all she saw in front of her was... the Sanctuary. She had a good view of the square from this height.

But I was facing away from it...

She turned around 180 degrees on the spot and tried walking away again – out towards the grassy hills. But that strange gentle nudging happened again, and all she was doing was walking back towards the Sanctuary. She tried again and again, but it was like there was an invisible bubble-like wall; when trying to walk into it, your shoulder slides along its flexible curvature and there is nowhere else for your feet to go, but to the side.

Evie growled to herself. All that was ahead of her was the Sanctuary. The rooftops of houses and shops, the narrow winding streets, and all the trees lining them. She could see roads leading towards a beach on the distant side of the square, and larger buildings she assumed to be the Museum and Art Gallery and so on. It was all just the Sanctuary as far as the eye could see.

Then suddenly, something violently grabbed both her arms. She saw a flash of two or three figures dressed in black – masks and gloves and all. She felt herself being lowered down onto something hard. And since that's the last thing she knew, I'll fill you in on the rest. The hard thing was a carrier-bed. There were four people carrying it – one on each corner, and they trotted her off down the hill again, back into the happy little village.

CHAPTER

ENTER OR EXIT?

Evie had made several attempts to open her eyes, but her eyelids were like heavy weights. When she could finally lift them, she saw that same ceiling with the same horrible light beaming down on her.

"Good morning," said a cold, trebly, weedy voice.

Evie jumped and turned her head to see a suited man sitting next to her in a chair. He was wearing glasses, had black thinning hair, and was resting a clipboard on his lap.

Evie realised she was in a chair like at the dentist – half sitting up, half lying down. She tried sitting herself up, but she didn't seem to have control over her limbs yet.

"Lay back and relax D14," said the man. "It's for your own good. If you try and get up, you'll only go and hurt yourself."

Evie tried to speak, but even her voice wouldn't work yet.

"My name is Mark." He glanced at his clipboard. "Now, D14, why did you try to escape?"

Evie just frowned and moaned a little.

Mark leant to one side where some controls on Evie's chair were. He slid one little knob along about two centimetres. "I think you'll find you can speak now," he said with a smile that never reached his eyes.

Evie cleared her throat gently. "I didn't."

"Why did you try to escape, D14?"

"I mean... I was just..."

"What were you doing so far from the Square?"

"I was walking."

"Why so far?"

"I felt like a nice long walk."

"Why is that?"

"I don't know. To get away from the people."

"So you were escaping, weren't you?"

"Well..."

"Weren't you, D14?" It felt like she'd gotten in trouble at school.

"I suppose. But how can you escape from a

place that everyone says they've escaped *to*?"

One of the man's eyebrows rose. "Why did *you* come here, D14?"

"I didn't come here. I think I was kidnapped."

The man did a soft, gentle, sinister laugh. "I'll ask again. Why did you come to the Sanctuary?"

"I don't have a reason. It wasn't my choice to come. I was brought here."

"By whom?"

"I haven't got a clue. Maybe that man, that... A1, I don't know."

"D14, people come here because they need to get away from their previous lives. An escape, as you put it. Now why do you suppose you're here?"

"I told you, I don't know."

"How about school? Your friend Tanya perhaps..."

"How do you know about Tanya?"

"Are you fed up with your friends? The way they bully you?"

"They don't bully..."

"Blackmailing," Mark interrupted, "is a form of bullying."

Evie swallowed and felt a lump there in her throat. "How..."

"Tanya found out you'd cheated in a test and now she's using the fact that you want to keep it a secret to make you do things you don't want to do."

The lump in Evie's throat grew, barring any further words from being able to get out.

"And now you feel distant from *all* your friends. Lashing out at them..."

"It's not *their* fault."

"No. You're just angry at yourself. And you need someone to understand but... there's no one."

Evie frowned, and felt a tear welling up.

"You wanted a kind word from your other friends, but Fiona just said..."

"You shouldn't have cheated in the first place," Evie said it with him, distantly.

"And that's not what you needed to hear is it? You already knew that. All you wanted to know – all you needed to know, was that somebody understood how you were feeling now. And help you in some way. To move forward."

"Yes," Evie turned to her side to face Mark.

"You wish there was a way you could avoid telling your parents; they'll just be angry and disappointed with you and make things ten times worse."

"Yes."

"And you're anxious about having to stand up to Tanya when you return to school."

"Yes!" Evie said.

"You don't have to stand up to her."

"But..." Evie sniffed, "then she'll keep on controlling me..."

"No she won't. Not if you're not there."

"What?"

"You don't have to see her again. *Or* your family. You can escape it all. Is that what you'd like?"

"Yes," Evie sighed again. She thought deeply of her family. School. Thin friendships.

"You can leave it all behind D14. Forget it all. Live completely... stress free. That's what you want, isn't it."

Evie thought of the times she'd laughed 'till her stomach hurt with her closest friends. When Fiona had stuck up for her in Grade Five. She thought of her Mum's hugs... Dad's laugh... her brother's jokes. She looked back sharply at Mark. "Of course not! I still love my family, and I can't give up on my friends!" She felt power in her arms and legs suddenly, propelled herself out of the chair and stormed out of the room.

Mark looked down sadly at his clipboard and put a big strike through the middle of the piece of paper resting on it. He then looked up in the general direction of a far wall and said out loud, "D14 interview unsuccessful."

Then came a different voice, in reply: "Let her leave. We'll see her again soon."

Evie recognised some of the hallways on her way out of that huge room. It was enough to find her way out of the building and once again, she was relieved to breathe in fresh air.

But it was sucked right back out of her again when she saw four men dressed in black trudging towards her. Evie was about to turn and run, but she quickly realised they were not here for her. They were dragging another girl towards the entrance of the Infirmary. She was tall, had mousy-brown tousled hair, and was kicking and pushing defiantly. On their way past, Evie and the girl's eyes met. And in that split second, Evie saw a slightly bigger glimpse of this place. Here was someone else they were about to interrogate, just like she had been. And all the while, nobody around was paying any attention to the commotion.

Evie knew then without a doubt, that there was something very very wrong about this place.

The Captain thought of Evelyn with discomfort. Imagined her being held as a prisoner. He was supposed to have taken her straight home, but one thing and another kept getting in the way.

"Don't get me wrong," said Asher. "It's not an actual prison where people go to receive a punishment for something bad they've done. They're being kept there for no reason whatsoever. No release date. No way to escape."

"So it's worse than a prison," Paulo said.

"*You* lot escaped," said the Captain.

"Well, very small chance of escape then."

"You still haven't told me how you managed it," said the Captain. "That's an awfully important point if we're hoping to get Evelyn out of there."

"Well the thing is," said Asher, "I've been thinking about the Sanctuary a lot lately. About all those people still living there. Most of them aren't even aware of what they're doing there and how they got there. We want to do something but..."

"But what?"

"There's always the thought in the back of my mind, that if we were to get ourselves back in there... to try and rescue people... we may not get out again."

"I see."

"But I believe that if we joined forces, had a proper team and an organised plan, we might have a chance."

"To get people out?"

"Surely yes, but we won't stop there! To over-throw A1's power. He's the man in charge. We'll take over the place and set *everybody* free!"

The Captain was speechless for a short moment. "That's quite ambitious."

"I know. And dangerous. But I would go in a second if I knew I had the right help."

The Captain considered and looked at Paulo.

Paulo shrugged. "We have to find Evie."

The Captain turned to Asher. "I'm game if you are. But I can't see how I'd be much help. I mean, you know far more about this place than I do."

"Just adding to our numbers may be help enough." He looked at Paulo. "Both of you I hope."

Paulo nodded. "I'm in."

After that, Asher met with everyone else, asking who would be willing to join them. Some were too afraid that they'd get stuck inside the Sanctuary again and wanted to stick to their original plan of finding a way off the planet. But a small few put their hands up. They ended up with eight in total.

The Captain and Paulo of course. Asher, tall, tanned and determined. Jon, another tall example of strength and fitness. Pintz, who was a shorter, stouter man with an honest face and the eyes of a loyal old sheep dog. Then there was Marnya, slim and fit, with smooth, spotless skin the rich colour of dates. She had long, shiny, flowing dark hair reaching down to the middle of her back. Roscoe, an older man whose hair was greying at the sides, but he looked just as fit as everyone else and had a kind smile. The last, was Elka, a woman with wispy, short, white hair, although she only looked about forty. She appeared to have a mild injury; she more sort of hobbled rather than walked.

"Are you sure no one else will come?" asked Paulo.

"Just us I'm afraid," said Asher. "And if we wait longer to give the others time to change their mind, I'm worried the ones we have will change *their* minds."

"It's now or never," said Jon.

"Come on, let's get going," Asher said to the newcomers. "I want to show you something."

They followed Asher, Jon and Pintz back across the countryside for ten minutes or so, with the others trailing behind.

"I assume you know where we're going," said Paulo, rather impatiently.

"Paulo," said the Captain, "don't be rude."

"This looks like where we started," he continued.

"Which means it's also where we saw Evelyn

disappear," the Captain pointed out.

"This is the place," said Asher. "This is where we believe there is evidence for the Sanctuary."

"What do you mean *evidence?*" the Captain asked.

"We think that it's in another dimension to this one. In the same place, but in its own..." Asher seemed to be searching for an appropriate word.

"Dimension?"

He nodded, "Well yes."

"Interesting." The Captain put his hands in his pockets and walked around the place.

"We're usually careful to stay well away from here," said Asher. "We've had disappearances like the one you described of your friend."

The Captain put on his glasses in a flicker of hope that something might show up through the lens. But nothing did of course. He did see the Train quite a distance off through the glasses – still standing proudly at the top of the hillside. He looked at it for a while, narrowed his eyes and then said, "I wonder..."

CHAPTER

THE CONSPIRACY

IIIIIIIIIIIIIIIIIIIIIIIIIIIIIIIIIIIIIIIIIIIIII

As a tall pencil of a woman called Sue in a grey skirt suit moved around her desk to approach another of her troubled clients, A1 was sitting in his oversized, over-computerised office, watching Evelyn passing through the streets on a huge screen mounted up on the wall. He jotted down some mental notes...

She's looking puzzled, disturbed, lost. Eyes darting everywhere, looking suspiciously at every simple thing. She's searching the faces of passersby. Probably looking for any sign of emotions like hers. She's going in circles. She doesn't know where she's going. She's seen someone, recognised them? She's walking towards... a girl... 7B12.

"Oh, goody," A1 grinned.

...said Evie. "Are you the girl I saw being dragged into the Infirmary place earlier?"

The tall girl looked down at her. "Yes," she replied with hardly any expression. Untrusting perhaps. Cautious. "Who wants to know?" she added in the same manner, facing Evie square on. The roll of an American accent was evident.

"Sorry," said Evie, "I was just... wondering er... I was standing outside the Infirmary at the time."

"Yeah, I noticed you." There was a pause. "Who are you?"

"Ev... um, D14."

The girl's eyes did a quick dart about and then fixed back on Evie and narrowed a little. More silence rang, as though they were both waiting for the other one to say something. But it was the American girl who finally spoke next. "Well, if you don't mind, I'll be getting home. Have a nice day."

That was not what Evie was hoping for. "Excuse

49

me but... I'm new here and... well, you looked as though you didn't want to be going to the Infirmary and... I was running away from it." She moved closer towards her and said a little quieter, "Can you tell me what's going on here?"

The girl frowned, perplexed. "You're ah... you're *wondering*? What's going *on*?"

Evie nodded earnestly.

The girl looked around again discreetly. "I knew deep down you looked different."

"Different?"

"When did you get here?"

Evie shrugged. "I'm not sure exactly. I've been asleep a couple of times."

"And... you wanna know why you're here?"

Evie nodded again. "Yes, very badly. And how I can get out!"

"Shhh!" said the girl aggressively. "We can't talk here." Then she let out a big, exaggerated laugh and gently patted Evie on the shoulder. She spoke again, noticeably louder. "You must come visit me. I have a beautiful apartment. I'll help you settle in. You'll feel like you belong in no time!"

A performance, it was obvious to Evie. But why? And who was the audience?

"Your second question, I can't answer right at this

moment," the girl said once they were inside her small apartment. "But I can have a good crack at your first one."

"Why couldn't we talk in the street?" asked Evie, puffing from a steep walk uphill.

"Because you never know who might be listening of course." As she spoke in a half-whisper, she was still looking around cautiously, darting from window to window, peering out of them with a worried expression. "It's dangerous to talk at all."

"Why? Who is it we're afraid of?"

"Everyone. *Anyone.* You can't trust a soul."

"Why not?" Evie asked wide-eyed.

"Look, we haven't got much time. We've probably already been detected and there'll be people on our trail. So can you just keep your mouth shut and listen?"

Evie suddenly decided that perhaps *this girl* was who she should be afraid of.

"Now where was I?"

"You can answer my first question?"

"Oh yeah. What's going on here. Well... you were probably wondering why I was being dragged against my will into the Infirmary."

Evie just slowly nodded.

"On my way in, I spotted you and I guessed straight away. That's happened to you too, right?"

Evie shook her head.

"But... you said you were running..."

"Well, at least... I wasn't dragged in there. But I suppose it was against my will. I was out to it."

"Oh," the girl replied knowingly. "Well, when you've been here as long as I have and you don't conform to their ways, they don't bother keeping so many secrets from you anymore."

"What kind of secrets?"

"The *great* secret. That this place is a trap. Not a getaway luxury resort or an oversized retirement village as most people believe it to be. You tried to escape, yeah?"

"Well... I suppose I did when I think about it. I was also just curious to see how far this place goes on for. Then I came to a certain point where I couldn't walk any further."

"Useless. Nobody will ever just *walk* out of here. There's like a weird, invisible bubble encircling the Sanctuary. Impossible to penetrate. If you tried doing that, they'll say you tried to escape. And I don't blame you. But it's useless. How do I know? Because for as many weeks as I've been here, that's how many times I've tried to escape. Any plan you could think of – I've tried it. I've tried going straight through, I've tried going up and over, I've tried going down and under. But every time,

I've failed. Whenever you get close – as soon as you finally feel some kind of hope that you might just make it... there come the guys in black."

"I remember guys in black."

"All they do is bring you back to the Infirmary. For you and other newcomers, they knock you out with a... special kind of patch thing that goes on your arm. With me, they don't bother anymore, because I know what goes on."

"But all the bystanders...?"

"Oh they're not bothered. They're all either patched themselves or they're just content to stay out of it and stay happy."

"Don't they... patch *you*?"

"Oh I've been patched before. I've had my out-to-it moments. But it's a matter of staying wise and staying alert."

"And what about this not talking in the street stuff? Are there undercover cops on the street or something?"

"A1's men. Very possibly, but it's not only that. There's surveillance in public places. You know, cameras. Listening bugs. Who knows where they watch and listen from, but I know they do."

"That's horrible."

"You're telling *me*."

"So this A1 dude, he's the guy who spoke to me

at the café. He seemed... nice. Except maybe a bit creepy."

"If he seemed so nice, what made you think he was creepy? You can't be nice *and* creepy, can you?"

"The way he sort of 'popped' in and out. I look around and he's there. And I look away and then back again and he's gone."

"He's like that. He doesn't have magic powers or anything, but he thinks it makes him look enigmatic."

"Enig...?"

"Er, mysterious... unfathomable. But just remember he's the bad guy in all of this."

"Hang on a minute. How do I know *you're* not the bad guy?" Evie said, plucking up her courage. "You just said how I can't trust anyone. Why are you trusting me? And why should I trust you? I don't even know your name yet."

The girl looked sad. "I feel like I don't have a name anymore. 7B12 is my 'name' here. Sorry I didn't introduce myself properly. It's just that a name doesn't mean anything here." Her face seemed to soften and, in her eyes, Evie detected a sort of longing suddenly.

7B12 looked around cautiously again, then looked earnestly at Evie, right into her eyes, and said in a hushed voice. "My name's Laura. And I think I trust you because... well, when I caught a glimpse of you outside the Infirmary, I just knew you were different. I've come across many undercover guys – trying to make me trust them. But you're nothing like them. And if we're going to get anywhere, I reckon we just take a giant leap of faith and trust each other. Despite what I said earlier."

"Well, you have an honest face."

"D14, you can't be a successful double agent with a *dishonest* face can you?"

I don't know what to do, Evie panicked silently. *What if this is a trap? I just met this girl.*

What will you do by yourself?

I don't know! I have no ideas of how to get out of this place on my own.

You do need somebody...

Evie tightened her lips determinedly, took a deep breath in and out. *Right.*

You've decided?

To take the leap.

What do you have to lose?

If this is a trap, then I'll be no worse off than I am now – stuck and clueless.

But not alone.

She looked up at Laura and gave a little smile.

55

"My name's Evie."

Laura smiled back. "It's a pleasure to meet you, Evie. But we'll have to be D14 and 7B12 most of the time."

"Why is that? What's wrong with people having their proper names?"

Laura shrugged. "Form of control I guess. This way, we can all be catalogued, indexed and monitored. I keep thinking what's it all for? And I still haven't gotten to the bottom of that one. I keep expecting some awful thing to happen. For us to be released one by one unto to a terrifying monster for A1's entertainment or, I don't know, be used as slave workers for some sinister, evil project. But nope. Nothing happens. Nothing ever happens. We're just... kept. It's as if..." Laura broke off suddenly when she'd heard something.

"What is it?"

"Shhh." Laura spoke in a whisper that was hardly even audible. "I thought I heard a motorcycle."

"Motorcycle?"

Laura looked at Evie with eyes on full alert. "We're in trouble... They know."

CHAPTER

DÉJÀ VU

Déjà vu is that feeling you sometimes get that the current moment you're having, you've experienced before. You know full well that you *haven't* experienced the exact same moment before, but you can sense it so strongly that you even feel like you know what will happen next. It's most likely due to the *remembering* part of your brain sometimes getting over-excited and making your *thinking* part of your brain *think* it remembers something, and we then become conscious of the feeling of remembering. But then your *thinking* part of your brain quickly works out that it's not possible for you to have experienced this exact same moment before, and then lets you know that the *remembering* part of your brain just made a botch-up of its one job. The 'remembering' feeling passes, you say to the nearest person who happens to be there, "I just got déjà vu!" and life goes on as normal.

If the *remembering* feeling *doesn't* go away by any chance, then you either need to get your frontal cortex checked out by a doctor, or you *have* indeed experienced the exact same moment before... which is creepy, so you should get yourself checked out anyway. But probably not by a doctor. More like someone who knows about time travel or extraterrestrial matters. The Captain, in fact, might be able to help you, but I'm afraid I don't know where he is right at this moment.

Now, we sometimes say we're having déjà vu when we find ourselves in *similar* situations, but this is not called déjà vu. This is called *being in a similar situation.* People also often say they're feeling a sense of déjà vu when they're actually just having to put up with something for the twentieth time.

At the time *this* story took place, (the one about the weird place called *The Sanctuary.* Remember?) the Captain had been rustling around in the Train for at least ten minutes, searching all the surfaces, looking under the floor, and fossicking through drawers. Paulo was waiting outside with Asher and the others.

After what felt like ages, the Captain emerged from the Train, saying, "Ta-daa!" and holding up what looked like a magnifying glass. His pockets also seemed to be noticeably bulkier. He strode over to Paulo and said with a smile, "I haven't used this in ages! It's been very useful to me on occasions in the past... and in the future come to think of it."

"A magnifying glass?" As soon as Paulo said it, he knew instantly that it wasn't just a magnifying glass. He noticed that it had a big dial and buttons and switches on the handle.

"Correction," said the Captain, "it's a Dimensionally Versatile Ocular Portal Lens."

Even though this sounded to Paulo, yet again, like one of the Captain's over-complicated gadget names, he did understand some of the individual words. "Dimensionally... versatile... do you mean, we might see things that are in different dimensions?!"

"Emphasis on *might.* I can't always tune in to the right dimension." The Captain was twiddling the dial on the handle – clockwise, anticlockwise. "I'm setting it to show me this very spot exactly one hour in the past." He then held it up in front of his face and looked at Paulo. For Paulo, the Captain's bulging pupil and speckled blue iris filled the lens. From the Captain's point of view, through the lens, everything was the same, except Paulo was not there.

"Good, it's working," said the Captain. "Now I just have to get it on the right setting..."

"Captain," said Asher impatiently, "you said you had an idea..."

"We've been here ten minutes, and you've done nothing," said Pintz.

"Nothing?" The Captain said in an offended tone. He turned to Paulo and muttered, "They're an impatient lot aren't they."

"Yes but, Captain," Paulo replied in a hushed voice, "Do you know what dimension the place is in, in order to see it in your... Dimensional... thing?"

"No. So I'm just going to have to try all the frequencies. And *they're* going to have to be patient."

From then on, Paulo seemed to become the Captain's messenger man, transmitting his explanations to Asher's mob in slightly more understandable words.

"The Captain has some tools that he's going to experiment with to try and locate the Sanctuary."

"What's he doing?" asked Marnya, obviously

not impressed yet.

The Captain kept twiddling the dial, pressing buttons and looking through the glass. Sometimes he would walk around with it, stooped over, looking just like Sherlock Holmes. Minus the hat. After a while, he 'tutted' to himself and muttered, "It's going to be the last one I try, I just know it."

"What's supposed to happen?" asked Pintz.

"I think he can see different dimensions through the lens," Paulo said.

Pintz looked curiously at Asher.

Paulo then whispered to the Captain, "Just how many dimensions are there to sort through?"

"Well, there's a theory that they're endless."

Paulo's eyes widened. "You mean infinite?"

"Yes."

"That's hard to fathom. How do you expect to find the right one?"

"I don't really. But it's worth a try." He gave Paulo an optimistic grin, and as he looked up to do the grin, it rapidly turned into a frown. He muttered a word – a name, that Paulo wasn't expecting. "Evelyn."

"Where?!"

"No, sorry, not Evelyn herself. That chap over there. Ross."

"Roscoe."

"That's the chap."

Paulo paused for a moment. "What about him? And what does he have to do with..."

"I'm getting déjà vu."

"What?"

"Well not *actually* déjà vu, it's just a similar situation."

"What's déjà vu?"

"Déjà vu is that feeling you sometimes get that the current moment you're having, you've experienced before. You know full well that you *haven't* experienced the exact same moment before, but you can sense it so strongly that you even feel like you know what will happen next. It's most likely due to the *remembering* part of your brain sometimes getting over-excited and making your *thinking* part of your brain *think* it remembers something, and we then become conscious of the feeling of remembering. But then your *thinking* part of your brain quickly works out that..."

"I think I understand, Captain," Paulo interrupted, looking worriedly at Roscoe. "That's exactly how Evelyn was acting just before she disappeared."

"Yes exactly."

They quickly rushed over to Roscoe, who had wandered a little way from the group.

"What is it, Captain?" called Asher.

"Somebody help us to wake Roscoe up!" he shouted. "Roscoe!"

"This place is beautiful!" said Roscoe in reply.

"Roscoe! Come back!"

It was too late. A blinding light engulfed Roscoe and the Captain and Paulo could get no closer to him. They all cowered from the light and the screeching sound.

When it fell quiet again, when they could finally look up to see what had happened, Roscoe was gone, of course.

It was about that time (relatively) that Evie and Laura were also about to experience a feeling of *déjà vu.* All Evie knew, after they'd heard the motorcycles, was that she had to follow Laura. They were soon out the door and running along another hilly lane that wound around and up towards a forest of trees.

She was already out of breath and tried to ask, "Where are we going?"

"Just run to the trees for some cover!"

When they'd reached the first few trees of the forest, they had climbed quite a steep hill and could see from a height the area they had just come from. Laura quickly ducked behind a thick tree trunk and whispered out harshly to Evie, "Get behind that other tree! Do you want them to see you?"

"Where are they?"

"They'll come, trust me."

There was that word again. *Trust.* Evie's mind was spinning.

"I told you it was unsafe to talk in the street. They probably suspected as soon as we laid eyes on each other."

Just as Evie was getting her breath back, she saw movement down by the apartments. Four men in black were marching straight for Laura's front door.

"There they are!" Evie whispered and turned to run.

"Don't move! Not yet," said Laura. "We'll wait 'till they've gone inside."

They watched in silence, until the men disappeared around a corner.

"That's our cue," Laura said, and she turned to run further up the hill, deeper into the trees. Evie's legs were burning from the climb. Her blood was running hot, yet her skin was cold from the chill air. The trees were all organised in neat rows and, oddly, they were lined with those same tall old-fashioned streetlamps.

"Where to now?"

"We keep to the forest," Laura said. "Safest place. They don't have surveillance in the forest. That I know of."

Laura kept running and Evie pushed past the pain in her legs, glancing suspiciously up at the streetlamps. While looking up, she tripped over a fallen tree branch, letting out a little yelp of surprise. Laura stopped, turned back to help her up, and it was then that they heard the motorcycles again. The girls looked with dread at each other.

"They're back on the move," said Laura.

"Does that mean we've lost?"

"Means we gotta run faster. Come on."

They ran side by side, until Laura took a sharp turn to the right. Evie turned quickly to follow her, but the sound of a bike seemed to come from that direction now. She turned back to the left, but then heard a second bike. The guys in black had separated to come rounding them up on both sides.

"Laura!" Evie cried out. She felt the vibration of the engines through the ground, off the trees. She caught a glimpse of Laura suddenly – on lower ground a little way off. She saw one of the bikes speeding up to her from behind and gasped loudly. "Laura!!"

The rider skidded, pivoting on the bike's front

wheel, thrusting a whirl of fallen leaves into the air. He landed right in front of Laura, and before she had a chance to change direction, the man in black was off his bike and grabbing her.

Evie realised she was on her own. *What did Laura say? The forest. Keep to the forest. It's the safest place...* Evie looked around desperately. She was *in* the forest! *Where's the next safest place?!*

The second bike was closing in. She kept her feet running, but she couldn't tell which direction the bike was coming from; the sound seemed to bounce off the trees and trick her all the time. *Bounce. Bounce. Bounce,* went the sounds all around her. And there it was.

The bike was dead ahead, speeding towards her. When she changed direction, the expert pursuer cut off her line of escape before she could blink. She dodged quickly again, but this time, her foot slid on the damp mushy leaves under foot, and she landed with a heavy thud on her stomach in the dirt. Strong hands grabbed her under the arms and yanked her to her feet. Hands like metal clamps, she had no hope of wriggling free. Soon, she was with Laura again, and the two of them were taken all the way back on foot to the Infirmary.

Once inside, they were split up. Laura tried to

yell out, "Stay alert! Don't let them..." The rest was muffled as a gloved hand came over her mouth.

It wasn't long until Evie was back on that chair in that room, with 'Mark' and his clipboard.

"Why did you run?" his voice echoed off the cold, clinical walls.

"Maybe because someone was chasing us," she replied obstinately.

"Were you trying to escape?"

"No. But if that happened, I wouldn't have been disappointed."

"Why did you seek the Sanctuary?"

"I didn't. I was brought here against..."

"What is your affiliation with 7B12?"

"I don't know what affiliation means."

"Why were you conversing with her?"

"Because I felt like it."

It went on. Evie was never sure what the right thing was to say. The only thing she had to go on was, *'stay alert!'* Because of Laura, stubborn boldness was bubbling up inside her. Sidling up beside the fear.

She hoped she was doing the right thing.

CHAPTER

VANISHING POINT

IIIIIIIIIIIIIIIIIIIIIIIIIIIIIIIIIIIIIIIIIIIIIIIII

"He's gone!" shouted Maryna, staring at the spot where Roscoe had been standing. "We were stupid to come to this place!"

"That's exactly what happened to my friend," the Captain told them. He strode over to the area. Paulo started to follow. "No Paulo, you'd better stay here."

"Captain, you can try all you like but I'm staying with you. Don't you remember the rule?"

"What rule?"

"The rule you set. I'm to stay with you. And I'm not accustomed to breaking rules."

"Oh yes... blasted rules. Okay then, come on." The Captain got busy on his various gadgets, trying to get readings. Paulo beside him, but the others keeping their distance. "He said 'this place is beautiful'. Evelyn said things like that. There could be some properties in the atmosphere, or... or in the grass or these flowers..." He squatted down and inspected the ground.

"What about the Dimensionally Versatile Ocular Portal Lens?" asked Paulo. "Have you gotten it to work?"

"It seems to react to one particular frequency, but I still can't see anything through it. As if someone's deliberately hiding the Sanctuary using a dampener of some sort."

"Well, I hate to state the obvious but... what about the Train?"

"The Train needs coordinates," the Captain picked a blade of grass and examined it. "Not only longitude and latitude, but dimensional. And I'm not sure I even want to take the Train in."

"Not take the Train? Why?"

"It could get stuck there. Just like we could. And Evelyn has."

"And now Roscoe."

"Or it could get confiscated. Destroyed. We don't know *what* we'd land ourselves in. *But...* it might be better if we're protected inside the Train for that very reason."

"What do you think, Captain?" Asher called, stepping towards them. "Can we get in or what?"

"It's feasible. Don't come any closer though. We're on very beautiful ground!"

Paulo looked at him oddly. "Captain?"

The Captain paused, shook his head. "I mean very *dangerous* ground. Have you thought of trying to get in the same way Evelyn and Roscoe did?"

"That's a terrible idea, Captain," said Asher.

"Is it?"

"Yes," agreed Marnya. "Go in that way and we'll immediately be captured. Probably put straight into the Infirmary."

"What's that?" asked Paulo.

"It's just a recuperating and treating clinic," said Jon. "But they do all sorts of sinister things in there. We certainly won't be any use from in there."

"My *word*," the Captain muttered, staring at the ground.

"What?" said Paulo. "Have you found a clue?"

The Captain stooped over to pick a wildflower. "Isn't that gorgeous!" Then he looked all around and squinted in the sunlight. "What a perfect place for a picnic or something."

"Oh no you don't! Captain!" Paulo shook the Captain's arm.

He blinked a few times. "Sorry? What is it?"

70

"We're not here to enjoy the wildlife! You're supposed to be examining the effects of the area!"

He blinked again and looked at Paulo like he'd only just appeared in front of him. Then he patted him on the shoulder. "Yes of course. Thank you."

"Can we get away from this spot?" said Paulo.

"Yes, I think we better had." He strode quickly back over to the others. "I'll have to think of something else. We could try and mark out the boundary of it using the frequency the portal lens reacted to, but of course that would..."

"Just a minute," said Elka. "Where's your friend got to?"

"Evelyn? We said... she's probably in the... but you already know that..."

"No no, *Paulo*. You left him behind."

"He was just..." The Captain looked around. Paulo wasn't by his side anymore, as he had just promised confidently that he would be. He had stayed back down the hill, and he was now staring up at the clouds.

"Paulo! No!"

And it happened again. The flash of light. The screeching sound. All over in a matter of seconds. Their group of eight, was now down to six. And the Captain felt the weight of it all on his shoulders, pushing down hard. "Right," he said with a heavy sigh. "We'll just have to do it the easy way then."

"You mean the hard way," said Asher.

"No I mean the easy way."

Asher looked astounded and impatient. "What do you mean the easy way?!"

"It could very well be the hard way at the same time. And so long as this frequency is giving the right coordinates. If you'll all come this way please." The Captain led the group reluctantly back across the hills. Back towards the Train.

When Paulo managed to get his eyes open, all he could see was a high, blurry ceiling and a white florescent light buzzing down on him. He blinked a few times and tried to sit up, but his head swam. He soon realised he was in a white bed, with white sheets and a white blanket. When his head stopped spinning, he looked around and saw the other empty beds and the ugly yellow and orange curtains.

"And how are we feeling, C36? All rested and ready to begin the day?" came an echoed voice.

"...Pardon?"

"And what a lovely day it is, too."

He tried standing up.

"Can you manage?" A woman in a nurse's

uniform approached him and went to help him up.

"Yes, I can manage I think." He stood up alright, but he was a bit wobbly. "Where am I?"

"Don't worry yourself about it. You're in safe hands now. You'll be well taken care of."

"Yes, but where am I?"

"The Infirmary," she replied as if it was a silly question. "Let me just take you to..."

"Where's Roscoe?"

"Roscoe? I don't know what a Roscoe is, I'm sorry. Just come along with me. You'll feel..."

"He must be here!"

"Anything wrong 317?" another voice from the entrance boomed.

"This one appears to be having difficulty."

"Well take him to the Recovery Room. Give it an hour. And if he continues in that way... you know what to do."

"Yes, A12." Then the nurse spoke to Paulo while the older woman left briskly. "Come on C36, all your questions will be answered soon."

Paulo reluctantly followed her out of the room and through the drab corridors. "Why are you calling me C36? What's that all about?"

"Everything will be explained," replied the nurse in a calm voice, just as she opened a door for him.

As soon as Paulo passed into the room beyond, the door was closed behind him. The nurse, gone. He stood there for a moment, feeling a bit like an animal who'd just been lured into a cage. Then he looked out onto a room that was full of people who didn't really see him. Some of them were on the floor playing with children's toys, some squished up in a corner keeping to themselves and some just sitting in chairs, staring. And then... his heart raced and his skin turned clammy all over. In one of those chairs, staring straight ahead at the tiny particles of dust in the air... was Evelyn.

Paulo raced over to her saying her name... but she didn't respond. Her face was blank. "Evie?" he said softly. "It's so good to see you. Are you okay?"

Her eyes moved slowly to meet his eyes. But there was no change of expression. She could see him perfectly well, but Paulo's heart sank when he realised... she doesn't recognise me.

She blinked, gave an empty, care-free smile, and then stared straight ahead again.

"Oh Evie," he whispered in dismay. "What have they done to you?"

CHAPTER

DIMENSIONAL HOP

Paulo started pounding on the door of the Recovery Room. Nobody inside the room paid any attention. But thankfully somebody *outside* did eventually come, after he'd made his fists and throat hurt. It was the matronly looking woman from before who was referred to as A12. She looked stern and severe, Paulo's shouts died out immediately.

She said very calmly, looking down her nose at him. "What is all this noise about?"

Paulo swallowed. "I want to know what's happened to my friend Evie in there. She doesn't know who I am!"

"I know no person of that name." She went to close the door on him again, but he persisted.

"You must know her, she's right here!"

"That is D14. And you mustn't be alarmed. It's only a short-term side-effect of her treatment. All part of creating a happy life here in the Sanctuary."

"What treatment?"

"She'll be as right as rain in an hour or so."

Paulo frowned. He still wasn't satisfied. "Well can I at least take her out of this place?"

A12 seemed to consider his request for a short moment, and then replied, "Very well. But you'll have to be discharged yourself."

"How long will that take?"

"Well, I don't like it, but if you're feeling alright, you can go to the front check-in station to be signed out with written permission from me."

It was a long and tedious process but that all eventually happened. However, Paulo never found himself back with Evie. He was told she was being released and taken back to her home, but Paulo didn't know where that was. He was soon placed inside a green and pink car to be sent home too. He kept getting called C36, and he never got a chance to ask the questions he wanted to ask.

Paulo was taken to a door, which was one of several, all evenly spaced out along the front of a long building like a motel. On the door was the number C36 in silver plating. When he opened it, he was astounded to see an exact copy of his very own compact living quarters near the Satellite Training Complex back on Serothia.*

As you can imagine, he went through all the same routine as Evie had done when she'd arrived at her home. And he ended up feeling just as miserable and uneasy in what was usually his favourite chair. But for Paulo, it was worse, because he had Evie to worry about. He wondered whether those nurses had kept their word.

"What a curious little vehicle," said Asher as he and those who remained of his group entered the Train's engine room. "Clever way of keeping hidden."

"What, *being invisible*? Yes, I dare say it is," the Captain replied, with a hint of sarcasm. He cringed afterwards though. He was trying to give up sarcasm.

"What exactly do you plan to do from in here, Captain?" asked Jon.

"From in here," the Captain replied, "I plan to get in there. The Sanctuary. Hold that for me will

---

* This had been Paulo's workplace when he met the Captain. He was a maintenance worker up in the Satellite that had orbited his home planet.

you, please." It was his Portal Lens that he wanted Jon to hold, so that he could use both his hands to work the controls of the Train. He copied combinations of numbers from the readings on the lens and entered them into a computerised panel which was embedded amongst the many taps, gauges and pipes at the front of the Train's engine room.

"You mean this thing can hop between dimensions?" Jon asked.

"On my lucky days," he replied, not helping at all to gain the group's confidence. "Hold it still! If I get just one of these numbers wrong, we could end up on the moon... of a distant planet... in another universe... 2000 years in the future."

Asher sighed. "Are you sure you can get us into the Sanctuary?"

"I told you. If it's a lucky day. Although I'd prefer not to rely on luck. Would you mind if we all joined hands for a moment?"

Blank faces stared back at him.

"No? Can I just say a quick prayer myself then?"

"A quick prayer? What's the man talking about?" asked Pintz.

"Never mind. Already done it. Let's go!" He pulled a lever and suddenly the Train whirred into action. The passengers had to hang on tight while they heard a deep chuffing and puffing sound coming from the core of the Train.

chuff CHOOFETY CHUFF CHOOFETY
chuff CHOOFETY BANG! CHOOFETY
chuff CHOOFETY CHUFF CHOOFETY
chuff CHOOFETY BANG!

The sound grew louder than usual and the ride was bumpier than usual and the Captain had to shovel in more Carnane fuel* than usual. He figured this was a good sign, because the power needed to hop through dimensions is much greater than what's needed to simply hop through normal space.

There was a DING! from the control deck.

"Well, the water's nice and hot if anybody fancies a cup of tea," said the Captain, after he'd finished shovelling in the fuel.

"Surprisingly, nobody feels like a cup of tea just at the moment, Captain," said Jon, his own impatience beginning to boil just as the water was.

The Captain shrugged, "Suit yourself."

---

* A special type of fuel that the Train needs to be able to go. It looks like glowing lumps of coal.

It was a good thing no one decided to have a cup of tea anyway because the Train ride suddenly got a good deal bumpier. The passengers were jolted from side to side, just as though they were on board an ordinary steam train running along a track.

"Is this normal, Captain?" asked Pintz.

"Perfectly! ...I think. Just have to materialise. It might be a bit of a fiddly business, so could you all keep very quiet now please?"

Down by the beach at that moment (relatively speaking), there were people either sunbathing, splashing in the water, or dozing off on their fold out beach chairs. And suddenly, there was a

chuff CHOOFETY CHUFF CHOOFETY
chuff CHOOFETY BANG!

getting louder and louder until suddenly, it stopped and there was a great, huffy sigh, with the **bubbling** and **HISSING** of steam.

Then from out of nowhere on a rocky mound near the water, came a man dressed in baggy brown trousers, a shirt with a knitted vest over the top and a train-driver's cap. He was followed slowly by five astonished looking passengers.

As soon as Asher, Jon, Pintz, Manya and Elka were on solid ground, the Captain turned and locked the carriage door. "Does this look familiar?" he asked.

"Yes," replied Asher, with dread in his voice. "This is the Sanctuary alright. See how nobody has even noticed us."

"Well let's just hope we *keep* going unnoticed," said Elka.

"I must admit," said the Captain, tucking his hands in his pockets, "It does look like a lovely place."

"Yeah, well don't be fooled," said Jon. "The place is like an iron cage."

"These people aren't acting very much like prisoners," said the Captain.

"That's because they're all controlled like puppets. A1 has them all on strings. Even their feelings are controlled."

"What a pity. Looks like nothing could ever go wrong here."

"Think again," said Asher. "All A1 has to do is pull one of his strings and..."

There was, at that moment, a loud scream from out in the water. They saw splashing and struggling about a half a mile out. The Captain ran up to the water, ready to dive in to save someone, but he quickly saw that there were three or four other people out there already doing it.

No. Not saving... the Captain realised, looking closer, *...restraining.*

They were all dressed in black and once they had a good hold of the woman in the water, they swam her back to the shore.

Asher tugged the Captain away. "We don't want to be noticed, remember?"

Unfortunately nobody reminded Elka of that. She recognised the person in the water. "That's J17," she mumbled. "She's my friend..." Before anyone could stop her, Elka rushed out from behind the new arrivals and towards the shoreline. "Take your hands off her! Leave her alone!"

And... they did. The people in black placed J17 down on the sand, motionless, and now one of them was walking straight towards the hobbling woman.

"Elka!" the Captain called.

"Shush!" Asher said, tugging at him again.

Elka collided into a man dressed in black. He stuck something on her arm and soon she went limp into his waiting arms. Meanwhile, the other three were lifting J17 onto a stretcher bed. And both her and Elka were carried away from the scene.

Everything on the beach kept going on as normal. In fact, everyone there had been going on as normal the whole time. It was hard for the

Captain to watch without jumping in to save the day. That's what he'd discovered he was good at.

"That's what would have happened to you, Captain," said Asher, "if you'd have tried to save the woman."

"Do you think she was trying to escape?"

"Likely."

"Aren't you worried about Elka?"

"Saddened. We know exactly what will happen to her now."

"She'll be taken to the Infirmary," Marnya explained tearfully, "questioned, interrogated, patched... and trapped here all over again. This was a bad idea."

"What does it mean to be patched?" asked the Captain. "Was that what was put on Elka's arm?"

"Yes," Jon said. "It numbs you to the realities of this place, numbs you from your need to fight back and be free. Properly free."

The Captain stared out at all the people on the beach, oblivious to what had happened. Oblivious to everything he guessed, and he pensively muttered, "Everyone knows nothing's doing. Everything's closed like it's a ruin. Everybody here is half asleep. We're on our own. We're in the street."

"Pardon?" said Asher.

The Captain snapped out of his thoughts. "They've got to be stopped. This is totally unethical."

"That's the spirit!" said Asher. "That's what I've been waiting to hear."

"Just one thing before we continue."

"What is it?"

"It's a question you still haven't answered."

"Well go on."

"If that's what happens when you try and get out of this place, how did you all escape?"

"Well... There's a different story for each one of us. A combination of coincidence, skill, know-how, and imagination. I'll tell you more about it on the way. Shall I show you where A1 lives?"

"Yes," said the Captain, narrowing his eyes slightly. "Lead on." The weight pressing on his shoulders felt heavier still. Now they were down from eight to five. And how long would it be, until they were down to four?

CHAPTER

10

FINDING EVIE

Paulo had been straight out of his apartment and on a search for Evie. On his way past the door, he saw the letter and numbers 'C36' and remembered that's what they kept calling him. *What did they call Evie? 14 something... what was the letter? Sounded like Cee, but a different sound... Mee? Bee... Kee... Dee... YES! It was D! 'D14'.*

Paulo's rush of excitement quickly sank back down again. How was he supposed to find a house or apartment or whatever it was, numbered D14? The map they'd provided looked like it was only a zoom up on the centre of the village.

He noticed all the doors near his apartment had 'C-something' on it. He wondered if people's houses were organised in letters. Perhaps this was the 'C' area, and not far away might be the 'D' area!

After a brisk walk, he soon discovered he was right. He came across lots of houses and units that now had 'D' on them. And although being organised, the buildings all seemed very mismatched. An unpredictable neighbourhood of hotchpotch. Different cultures, different designs, different styles everywhere you looked.

When he finally found the number 'D14' on a white box attached to a little wooden pole, he rushed up to a one-storey house beyond, past a yard covered in fallen leaves. It looked strange to Paulo because he wasn't from Earth, but to you and me, it would have looked like a very average house, perhaps just like yours.

He sped up to the front door and knocked urgently. The door was answered, and he sighed in relief. "Evie!"

"Hello. How are you? Would you like to come in?" she said, all in one breath.

Paulo's brow twitched into a frown. He slowly followed her inside, looking at her curiously. "You... *do* know who I am, don't you?"

"Of course I do," she said, smiling. "You're C36. I saw you in the Recovery Room. And I'm told it's thanks to you that I'm out of there so early."

"...Yeah." Then he whispered to her, "Obviously it's dangerous to talk or something, is it? I've kind of gathered that the people in charge here are rather... controlling."

"People in charge? Controlling? What are you talking about? And what is... Evie?"

"What is this place? I know it's called the Sanctuary, but what goes on here? Why have we been... wait, what did you say?"

"The Sanctuary is a place to... to relax. To chill out. Be away from the stress of life."

"Are you being serious?"

"Of course. I don't think I've ever felt happier."

"But Evie!"

"My name is D14," she frowned. "What exactly do you want? I can get some milk and biscuits. Or do you want some tea? I can make some tea."

She started walking towards her kitchen, but Paulo grabbed her by the wrist and stopped her. "Snap out of it, Evie! Wake up! How do we get out of here? There must be a way out!"

"Why would you want to leave?" Evie asked. "This is the coolest place ever! No school, no homework, no one telling us what to do..."

"But don't you see Evie? You're not meant to be here. This isn't your life. What about the Captain? What about your family back on Earth?"

Evie slowly frowned. "...Earth?"

I have to do something, Paulo thought with a pounding heart. And I think I'm on my own.

On your own?

I can't rely on the Captain and Asher and the others. They may never even make it inside.

Perhaps I should try to get out again...

But you just got in. You were trying to get in and now you're in.

But the Captain would know what to do.

But you *literally* just got in. I just spent the last hour getting at least *someone* else inside.

Well I don't know what to do now I'm here I... wait... can I hear...

Yes, it's just me.

Well... maybe you could give me some clues.

I'm often trying.

Do you know what's going to happen?

Well, I find it's much better when...

Do you know how it ends?

Just... get on with what you were about to do... however silly I think it is.

"You stay right here," Paulo said to Evie, and rushed out of the house.

Evie was left alone, watching him disappear down the lane. She smiled thoughtfully to herself, then wandered over to her telephone. She dialled a simple letter-and-number combination. *A – 1.*

"Yes D14?" a calm, male voice answered.

"You know C36? The newcomer?"

"Yes."

"He's going to try and escape. Probably on his way through the square by now."

"Thank you very much, D14."

CHAPTER

11

AND THEN THERE WAS ONE

||||||||||||||||||||||||||||||||||||||||||||||||||||||||

Paulo really had no idea how he was going to get out. But the most logical thing to do was to run to the surrounding hills, as far away from the main part of the Sanctuary as he could. Maybe it would be as simple as crossing a border.

> I might be out already.
>> Ha ha haaa... Oh, that's a good one.
>>> I must be out.

Newcomers. They're so adorable. You can keep running. But you can't escape.

> Can you think of something useful?

Escaping's not my plan. And perhaps you should stop running because you're about to...

His body was suddenly flung backwards onto the grass. He lay on his back, dumbfounded, staring up at the sky. If it happened to you, you might say that it felt like colliding into the wall of a jumpy castle.

Paulo sat up. He saw nothing in front of him, but perhaps it was like the Train... only soft. He lifted a hand to try and feel for whatever it was, but he didn't get a chance to find out. The loud sound of motors arrived. Two cars, both with no roof. One had four people, all in black, jumping out of it carrying a stretcher bed, and the other had a man of middle age in the driver's seat. He was balding and had a rosy bulbous nose. Next to him, in the passenger's seat, was Evie.

"That is A1's control centre," Asher said to the Captain after the group had come through the Sanctuary Square from the beach. "We think we can get to the bottom of all this if we can get in there."

They were looking up at a big round building, its curved concrete walls reaching up to the sky. It was hard to tell how many storeys because there were hardly any windows. Just one line of tiny windows high up around the circumference near the top, making it look like an oversized watchtower. At ground level, there was one large glass door at the front, and coming out from the doorway towards the street was a wide path lined with neat, trimmed plants. Where the path joined the road, there was a big, tall gate, keeping people out (unless they had a combination to the little keypad, which was mounted onto it).

Asher pointed out the surveillance cameras that surrounded the building, as well as one that was right at the main entrance.

The Captain said finally, "Are you expecting me to find you all a way in?"

"No," replied Asher. "You have done your job of getting us back in here undetected..."

"As far as we know," said the worried Marnya.

"Now it's our turn," continued Asher. "I'm glad to say that we should be able to take it from here."

"During our time here," Pintz explained, "we managed to devise a way of getting into that building unnoticed. Those cameras have a blind spot. If we can all remain unseen by them, the rest is easy."

"What do you mean?" said the Captain. "We still have a twenty-foot-tall gate to get past. Now unless you know the combination, I can't see..."

"But that's just it, Captain," said Jon. "We do know the combination. When Asher was brought here once for interrogation, he saw the guard punch in the number!"

"Wouldn't the guard have been more careful than that?"

"I was supposed to be unconscious at the time," said Asher. "But they clearly hadn't given me a strong enough patch."

The Captain paused and frowned. "...Wouldn't they have been more careful than..."

"Asher," said Pintz.

"What is it?"

"I think I know how we're going to get inside. Look!" There was a man in white overalls with a trolley full of boxes, walking in the direction of the huge round building.

"Looks like a delivery," Asher said, happy astonishment in his tone. "Right, we've got no time to lose. The blind spot we were talking about. That delivery man will pass it soon and when he does, we'll be there waiting. We'll knock him out, I'll dress in his overalls and you lot can hop in the trolley. Covered in all those boxes, there's no way you'll be seen."

"Are you sure about this?" asked Marnya.

"Of course. It's too good a chance to pass up. And if we wait any longer, we won't have to pass it up, it'll pass itself up. Who's with me?"

Jon and Pintz agreed nervously and Marnya,

exchanging glances with the Captain, also anxiously agreed. The Captain generally preferred to go about things *without* knocking anyone out. But he reluctantly shrugged. "Well if anyone knows this place it's you fellows. I can't wait to finally have a word with this A1 chap."

"We'll walk up casually," said Asher. "I'll lead, and bring you all to the blind spot."

They walked casually across a small parkland which was part of the Sanctuary Square, across a cobblestone road, and then to a little niche between a curved edge of the big, tall gate and the sharp right-angled corner of a giant brick building next door. There they watched and waited for the delivery man to approach.

"What's this place next door?" the Captain asked quietly.

"That's the Infirmary," said Asher. "This part of town is where it all happens. It's like the heartbeat of the Sanctuary." He stopped talking. "Shhh, here he comes."

When the delivery man walked past with a happy tune on his lips, Asher pounced out from hiding, gave him a sharp blow on the back of his neck and dragged him into their hiding spot.

"He's out alright, but he'll be fine in time. Quick, get into the trolley."

Soon, there was a delivery man in white overalls with a trolley full of boxes once again approaching the big, round building.

Beneath the boxes, Maryna whispered, "You're squashing my hand."

The Captain shifted quickly. "I *do* beg your pardon."

"Shhh," said Asher as he approached the gate confidently. He pressed the numbers in one after the other, without hesitation. The gate slowly slid to the left, leaving a wide-open space, with nothing ahead but the pathway leading all the way up to that large, glass door. When he was halfway up the path, the gates slid shut behind him, and when he stood at the door, it was opened to him. He entered with a huge grin on his face and from here, he knew exactly where to head.

From beneath the boxes, the Captain heard him say suddenly, "Delivery for A1."

Then a different voice said, "Just drop it here."

"I had instructions to take it directly to A1 himself," replied Asher.

"Oh... He'll be back soon. Wait here please."

"This is it," Asher said to the trolley when they were alone in the room. "What are you going to say to him, Captain?"

The Captain rose up from out of the trolley,

lifting the boxes and putting them aside. "I don't know yet. I usually just make it up as I go along."

"I can't believe I'm here again," said Marnya, stepping out of the trolley. "And in *this* place. A1's lair."

"Worried?" the Captain asked her.

"Very. I'm worried about what A1's going to do with us when he sees us."

The Captain looked around the room. He couldn't see anything that gave him clues as to how the place was run or how it might possibly be stopped. It was just a bare, circular room, like a foyer or grand hallway, with a shiny marble floor.

After five minutes or so, a man came into the room and said that A1 had returned and a grand door was opened to them. He didn't seem perplexed at all that there were now five people standing there, instead of one.

The Captain hadn't expected to be led straight to him. The grand door led into a short, grand passageway and there was another grand door at the end of it, which opened before them without anyone having to touch so much as a doorknob. In the large room beyond, there was an oversized desk with a big high-back, cushiony, black chair behind it in the centre of the room. The chair was facing away from the door and all that could be seen of the

person sitting in it was the top of a balding head. The chair slowly turned around and the enigmatic A1 was revealed in a suave, dramatic, way. He was quite ordinary looking. Nothing about his appearance was particularly frightening or sinister, but Marnya shivered and was filled with dread at the sight of him. Asher, Jon and Pintz waited hungrily for what he was going to say.

A grin came across A1's face slowly as he eyed each person standing before him in turn. And when he did open his mouth to speak, it was certainly not what the Captain wanted to hear.

"Thank you, gentlemen," he said coolly. He was looking directly at Asher, Jon and Pintz. "You have done splendidly. It couldn't have been easy luring this strong-minded troublemaker into my trap. He'll make a lovely addition to my collection." He laughed with excitement. And then Asher, Jon and Pintz walked forward to join A1 behind his desk.

"I'm not particularly interested in the girl," A1 went on. "You can send her to the Infirmary and she can be patched and taken back home. As I always say, there's no place like home."

While A1 was saying this, Pintz pushed a small button on one section of the desk and spoke into a speaker. "Can I have someone in here to take away a patient please?"

Both the Captain and Marnya were stunned. Marnya looked terrified. The Captain's nostrils flared. *How did I not see it?* he thought, angry at himself. *It was obvious all along... wasn't it?*

Within seconds, there was a man and a woman dressed in black who came and grabbed Marnya, one on each arm. She tried to clasp onto the Captain in protest, but they whisked her away, kicking and screaming. Her shouts grew quieter and quieter as she was quickly marched away.

"What is this?" the Captain asked through clenched teeth.

A1 merely sat there, contented. "Z23, would you kindly explain?"

It was Asher who spoke, evenly as always. "A1 first tracked you wandering about on planet Zero early this morning. He contacted me from the Sanctuary to..."

"To lie to me. All three of you are A1's agents. I must say you're good at your job. Usually I can detect liars quite easily."

"Ah, you admire their skill," said A1.

"*Admire* it?" The Captain had managed to contain his anger well. Until now. "It's an utterly and totally... appallingly... *horrid* thing to do. Haven't you learnt that liars don't go unpunished? There are not many things that cut deeper... than lies."

"Oh I'm sorry," A1 patronised. "Sorry that you appear to have lived such a sheltered life. Fancy never being lied to before. Perhaps you need to get out more."

"I didn't say I've never been lied to," the Captain said evenly. "I've had my share. And I've never managed to get through to the liar that it benefits them not one jot in the end."

"It's a shame you couldn't get any more of those poor lost souls out there to come with you," A1 said to Asher... *Z23*.

"We tried our best."

"Well we got three back. That's not bad to be going along with. And three new ones now as well!"

"What do you mean 'planet Zero'?" the Captain said. "Is that what this planet's called?"

"I've called it that," said A1. "Rather fitting don't you think? When one comes to the Sanctuary, they have zero worries, zero responsibilities, zero stress!" he smiled cheerfully.

"Yes and zero *life* by the looks of things. Why do you do it? Why are you running this place? And why have you gone to so much trouble to bring me here?"

"Ah, well *you* were an interesting case. At first, you were just another potential addition to my collection. But after Z23 and the others, 1F90 and E206 had started interacting with you, I decided to test you out. Work out what kind of personality I was up against. The original plan was merely to lead you close enough to the zone of dimensional proximity for it to snap you up, but I thought I would have a little fun with you first. Now I know more about you and now I can create a more appropriate stay for you here in the Sanctuary."

"And what do you mean by *collection*? What collection?"

A1 looked amused, as if the answer was obvious. "*My* collection." He leant forward. "Of people."

CHaPTeR

12

TIME FOR A CHECK-UP

IIIIIIIIIIIIIIIIIIIIIIIIIIIIIIIIIIIIIIIIIIIIIIIIIIIIIIII

Evie was eating some bread and jam at her quiet kitchen table, staring out the window. The outing she'd had with A1 had made her peckish. But now, her vacant smile began to drop, her chewing slowed. She looked up at the clock and couldn't believe her eyes. How could it have been three o'clock? It only felt like five minutes ago she was with Laura in her apartment. Something on the fridge caught her eye. It was a note on a business card-sized leaflet. It wasn't there before.

She pulled it off the fridge, looked at the clock again and realised the appointment time had passed. She couldn't even remember *getting* this little card from the Infirmary. But then, a picture flashed into her memory. A picture of that Recovery Room...

...and Paulo. *Paulo* had been there! She suddenly remembered that feeling. Of seeing him, but not being able to do anything about it. Not quite understanding who he was. But *now* she knew. Why couldn't she tell him back then?

She quickly checked her arms above the elbow, and sure enough, she found a little square of green plastic stuck to the skin of her left arm. She remembered what Laura had said about being 'patched'. She'd been a mindless sleepwalker like all the others for a short time and now she needed a top up because it was wearing off.

She screwed up the little card and threw it in the kitchen peddle-bin. Then, as if things couldn't get any weirder, she heard a brass band playing outside. Curious, she left the house to see what was going on. Again, the tune gave her unease. It was upbeat and bouncy, yet somehow shady and twisted, as though someone was making a mockery of happiness. When she reached the end of the road, she saw there was a short procession of people, all wearing black. In the centre of the procession, Evie saw that four people were each holding up a corner of a simple wooden coffin, and she got a start. *I suppose people do die here. An elderly person probably, died of old age...*

She stood there, watching them walk by respectfully, but then noticed a metal plaque attached to the side of the coffin that made her stomach squirm.

7B12. 7B12. 7B12...

The name went whirring around in Evie's head like a dizzying sandstorm. She forgot all about the procession and left, heading for the Sanctuary Square. Although she'd never wanted to step inside there again, she went storming into the Infirmary and shouted at the nurse behind the reception desk, "What happened to Laura?!"

"Laura?"

She huffed angrily, "7B12 then! Where is she?"

"Do you mean the *previous* 7B12?"

"She's been replaced?"

"Naturally. I'm afraid the previous 7B12 was sadly taken by erm... let me see..." the nurse looked through some records on a clipboard. "A speeding car. It was a tragic incident."

Evie's mouth went dry; she could hardly speak. "You mean... you mean she was hit?"

"Died instantly apparently. There was nothing the doctors could do I'm afraid." She spoke gently but somehow it was completely sympathy-deficient.

"I don't believe it," Evie said, half in a daze.

"You're due for a check-up, aren't you?" the woman said all of a sudden. "Let's see..." She was looking at another clipboard full of records. "D14. Half past two." She looked up sharply at Evie with a worried expression. "...You'd better come along with me."

Before the woman could get a hold of her, Evie was out of there like a shot. She knew what a 'check-up' would mean. She would be 'patched' again and sent into a dazed half-existence for the rest of the day. She couldn't let that happen again. Once outside, she didn't know *where* to run, but she was running anyway.

I could look for Paulo! Where would he be? What was his number? C36 – that's right! She would head for the 'C' houses... *if he's home...*

...But he's probably out looking for me.

She changed her mind. The words of Laura echoed in her head again. *Keep to the forest. Safest place. They don't have surveillance in the forest.*

Well, she didn't have a clue what she was going to do once she got there, but at least she could stop a while and think of a plan.

Evie realised quickly that she'd gotten away from the busy part of the Sanctuary just in time. She heard a cheerful voice over a nearby loudspeaker:

ATTENTION, SANCTUARY CITIZENS... ISN'T IT A LOVELY DAY! BE ON THE LOOK OUT FOR A RUNAWAY PATIENT WHO IS IN URGENT NEED OF CARE.

SHE IS A YOUNG GIRL OF ABOUT THIRTEEN OR FOURTEEN, HAS LONG BLACK HAIR, WEARING BLUE JEANS, PINK T-SHIRT, AND WHITE HOODED JACKET. HER NAME IS D14 AND IT IS

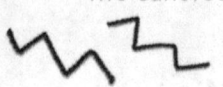

VITAL THE INFIRMARY HAS HER BACK IN ITS CARE. IF YOU SPOT HER, PLEASE INFORM THE AUTHORITIES AT ONCE!

Evie had never asked or even wondered what it was like to be a fugitive. But now, it was thrust upon her, with no instruction manual. No escape.

Paulo was sitting in a room lined with chairs with seven or so other people. None of them talked or even looked at each other.

A nurse came in. "B618?"

A man stood up and left the room with her. He was gone a while, and when he came out, he had a vacant smile on his face as he left.

"A67?"

This time, a woman stood up and followed the nurse out, just as though it was a mundane task of having a dental check-up. A few minutes later, she left with that same distant smile.

"K23?"

An older man stood up and went with the nurse. Another few people came in and sat down.

Paulo leaned to the person on his left. "What's

106

this for? What happens in there?"

"Just our check-up," the man next to him said.

Well, that wasn't helpful. The old man came out wearing a careless smile.

"C36?" the nurse called.

Paulo was careful to notice a small, bluey-green square sticker on the man's upper arm as he left.

"C36?"

That's the patch Asher and the bunch were talking about! Paulo thought.

"C36!" the nurse repeated, looking at Paulo.

Paulo looked back, wide-eyed. "Not me."

The nurse frowned. "But I'm sure... Let me just go and check." She exited.

"I'm getting out of here," Paulo stood and announced to the people left in the room. "This is not natural. Does anyone want to join me? There's not much time. Soon, that nurse'll come back realising C36 *is* me."

Some of the waiting people snuck glances at him, the way you might do when you notice someone odd out in public, and you don't want them to notice you noticing them.

Paulo frowned, second-guessing himself. Maybe they're doing a good thing here. Making people better... happier... But he couldn't get rid of the uncomfortable feeling in the back of his head – and it wasn't where the mosquito had bitten him a few days ago back in ancient Jerusalem.

He quickly rushed out of the waiting room and found himself in a corridor. He stopped abruptly, not knowing which way to turn, and also because running would look suspicious.

Left, or right?

He heard voices coming from the left.

Right it is! he thought, and paced down the hallway trying to look like he belonged. Unfortunately, the voices didn't get any quieter. Whoever they were, were following right behind him. He could hear them talking:

"I think I'll stay with him for a while and see what I can get out of him. What do you think Mark?"

"Yes, that's a very good idea, Mark. Where are the records from the last patient?"

"Right here, Mark"

"Thank you, Mark. I'll take those to A1."

Paulo frowned one eyebrow, perplexed, and certain they would catch up to him. He had to get out of sight. But again unfortunately, there was a dead end straight ahead, with only a series of closed doors all the way along the corridor. He was boxed in. He would have to try his luck with one of the doors. He knew that the one he entered might also be the one the two Marks wanted to enter, but he had to take the chance. He quickly ducked inside a door to his right.

He listened for the voices. They got louder... but thankfully, quieter again and then eventually faded altogether with the sound of a different door closing somewhere else nearby. He breathed a silent sigh of relief, then turned to see that he was faced with yet another corridor, lined with closed doors. But the lighting was dimmer, and a slight shade of red. Unease squirmed inside him.

The doors lining this corridor had little round windows in them, and Paulo couldn't resist sneaking a peek. He was careful at first, in case there were people inside. But when he caught a glimpse, he was so disturbingly mesmerised he couldn't look away.

He frowned a most bewildered frown as he stared into a dim, blueish-lit room with eight or so people inside. They were sitting on the floor around the edges of the room, their backs against the wall and their legs stretched out in front of them, laughing. As though they were learning how to laugh or trying out different kinds of laughs. It would have made Paulo laugh too if he didn't have that disturbing unease in the pit of his stomach while watching. He moved onto the next room. Another group of people were walking slowly in a line behind a smartly dressed woman in a skirt suit. They were following after her taking one slow step after another, calmly and carefully, as if they were just learning how to walk. Another room had a group of people sitting in a circle tearing bits of paper in synchronised rhythm as though timed to their heartbeats, and letting the pieces float to the floor...

A door opened somewhere around a corner. Paulo's stomach twanged. He heard voices again. Would he have to hide inside one of *these* rooms? He quickly worked out which direction the voices were coming from, and looked for an escape.

CHAPTER

13

THE COLLECTOR AND THE PROTECTOR

Normal people have rock collections, shell collections, keyring collections, or stamp collections. (The Captain had even known somebody with a letter box collection.) But a *people* collection? That had to be the most bizarre one he'd come across. Not to mention the most unethical.

By now, Asher, Jon, and Pintz (or rather Z23, 1F90 and E206) had left the Captain alone with A1. He paced around the huge desk of the huge, sumptuous office. "So, let me get this straight. The Sanctuary is basically a big storage place for your collection?"

A1 followed him with his gaze, slowly rotating

his swivel chair. "Oh, it's much more than that."

"What then?"

"It's a *paradise.* Where people can escape from life. People are so stressed, they've no time to rest and enjoy life's pleasures. And I'm sure I don't have to tell *you* how beneficial rest is."

"Of course, but rest must balance with work. There's a time for everything, A1. A season for every activity under heaven. Of *course* people want rest. But you can't do it all the time."

"You're wrong, Captain. People never want to go back to reality after a holiday. You ask anyone. Back to work, school, routine. Why do it when you don't have to? I'm saving these people. Offering them a permanent sanctuary."

"You're not offering it, you're forcing it on them whether they want it or not."

"Everybody wants it. Deep down inside, *everybody* wants a good, long rest. And it's not like my people do *no* work at all. They have jobs in the village as shopkeepers, taxi drivers, waiters and cooks. But it's all restful. They all enjoy doing it. I don't force them to work if they don't wish. Everybody you see doing something, they're doing it because they want to. They see it as a service back to me for what I have provided for them."

"Are you sure about that?"

"Of course. But you seem to be fixated on *them* on all *their* needs. And while I've done my best to make them happy, the Sanctuary is also about me... and *my* needs. You see, Captain, It's not just a collection, it's my passion. Interestingly enough, this place started out as a temporary holiday resort. And over the years I enjoyed hearing people's stories of why they chose to come, what made them decide to take a break, and they all... interested me. All those lives and motives for doing what they do. Over time, I realised that everybody needs a holiday, and I always hated seeing people go when it was time for their holiday to end. I saw their dread at the thought of going back to their lives... and I felt *my* sadness... when they left...

"I've developed a real hobby for collecting people now. The thrill of catching them. The challenge of finding new and better ways of luring them in. And then seeing the joy and happiness on their faces when they realise they have nothing to ever worry about ever again. It's priceless. And I wouldn't give that up for anything."

A1 got up and went to some controls that were embedded in one part of the curved wall. He pressed a button and a whole section of the wall slid back effortlessly, revealing a huge screen behind it. On the screen was live surveillance showing a

113

hallway of the Infirmary, and the Captain recognised Paulo straight away, walking cautiously down it.

"This young chap for example, resisting what I'm offering him here. He's just so interesting, don't you think? I'm glad I've got him. He makes for quite good entertainment. Look at him, wandering about in a staff-only zone."

The Captain pretended not to recognise him. "Aren't you going to catch him?"

"I want to see what he does first." A1 was watching as if it was his evening television viewing. The only thing missing was the popcorn.

Paulo looked as though he'd heard voices again and was wondering which way to turn, when an alert signal sounded there in the office.

"Ah!" A1 said cheerfully. "A new case by the sound of it!" He pressed a different button, and the screen changed from Paulo and the corridors, to what looked like another office – a consulting room with a suited man behind the desk, and a young lady sitting opposite him, saying:

"I feel so low at the moment, I just don't know what to do. I have so many things I need to do but I don't know where to start. I don't want to start at all, that's the problem. I just feel like going to bed, curling up with my head under the blanket and staying there, and for the whole world around me to just stop."

A1 was nodding and smiling. "Yes, yes, and so you shall, don't you worry. Sounds like she needs a sanctuary, wouldn't you agree, Captain?"

He wasn't given the opportunity to answer. A1 held a button down and spoke into a little microphone. "Mark, A1 here. Take your client into the Forgetting Room. Remember, *client,* not patient. Bring her to the Sanctuary. She'll love it!" He smiled, rubbed his hands together and skipped back over to his desk. "She'll be a lovely new addition. She *could* be a bit of a troublemaker, but we'll get her straightened out." A1 laughed greedily and started making some notes on a piece of paper at his desk.

The Captain couldn't get the frown off his face. He looked back at the big screen and watched as the poor girl was led into a little adjoining room. Then came a flash of light, and that screech that he'd heard when Evie was taken.

The sun was shrinking away behind the trees, behind the horizon, but Evie was too afraid to come out of the forest to go home. There didn't seem to be any danger here. There was plenty of light dolloped along the straight passageways of the forest thanks to the standing streetlamps. Evie had to admit, it was pleasant and peaceful. There was no sign of any night creatures, or even any creepy crawlies on the ground. But as calming and non-threatening as it was meant to be, it filled her with discomfort. It felt manufactured. She felt trapped. Perhaps even more trapped than before. Trapped, helpless, alone... and cold.

She sneezed suddenly and hoped she wasn't coming down with something. Her ears were ringing. The silence started to become like noise in her head. Moving was better because at least then she had the sound of her footsteps to keep her company.

Just as she found herself hoping not to come across any invisible bubbles again, she spotted a dark puddle of water on the ground. Her body, all of a sudden, told her how thirsty she was, but she squinted at the little pool suspiciously. The water looked black and, oddly, when she leant over it, there were no reflections.

She knelt beside it and dipped the very tip of her finger in. She pulled it out again, perplexed. Her fingertip wasn't wet. She dipped her finger in again, this time, plunging it in a little further and swirling it

116

around in circles. And when she pulled it out again, it was still dry. She also realised, her finger had made no ripples.

This is no ordinary pool, Evie thought, and as I'm sure you've probably guessed, it was certainly not water. When she placed her whole hand in, it felt like... nothing. Just as though she was moving her hand through air.

Another sneeze jumped up on her, which made her whole body spasm. So much of a spasm that she lost her balance and fell right into the p o o l . . .

...No splash.
...No wetness.

She was summersaulting, sideways along dry ground. When her body stopped rolling and she got back up onto her feet, she looked around, completely puzzled. She was still in the forest, or more accurately, still in *a* forest. But it had changed. It was much darker than before, and the sounds weren't so pleasant. She heard some creature somewhere nearby do its short spooky night call that sounded like a distressed scream.

Then she heard flapping of wings and imagined bats up in the trees. She looked back to try and see where she had come from, but couldn't recognise any of it. There was no sign of the streetlamps.

She did see a funny kind of tree. With a very huge distinctive hollow in the middle of its trunk. But strangely, it was not actually hollow. Inside the hole was just pitch black, like the pool had been. She poked her hand through the hole and it disappeared into the blackness.

"Some kind of... portal?" she said to herself, in disbelief. With hesitation again, she leant forward and put her head, face-down, through the hole this time...

And she saw the forest she was in before. Because she was looking straight down, she expected to see the forest floor, but what she actually saw was a regular view of the forest you would get if you were looking straight ahead. The old forest that she was standing in before was tipped ninety degrees. (Or was it *this* one that was tipped ninety degrees?) Anybody standing in the old forest would have seen a head protruding upwards out of the black pool Evie had fallen into.

She quickly pulled her head back out through the hole in the tree trunk and tried to fathom what was going on. Maybe she had just passed through a window from one dimension to another. *Maybe I'm out of the Sanctuary!*

She hoped it was not just wishful thinking. She knew that the two forests were definitely in different dimensions because of the weird ninety-degree angle. And she knew that *this* forest was dark and gloomy like a forest at night should be.

She felt a cold shiver run through her. Then there were footsteps, and she heard the panting of a very large, probably very dangerous animal. Big paws plodding along the leafy forest floor. The rustling of some foliage nearby. She started running. The footsteps of the animal also sped up. Galloping. What was it? A lion? A tiger? A bear?

"Oh my!" she shrieked, and ran faster. She came across a giant tree with another hollow in it. Only this was a normal hollow, near the base of the tree, and big enough for her fit inside. She climbed in, and a violent flutter of wings startled her. She wrapped her arms around her head and stopped herself from screaming. Once the wings had all flapped away, she breathed deeply in and out, leant her head against the back of the hollow and tried not to think about what creepy crawlies might be hiding in there with her.

Then, in that cold, musty and lonely tree trunk, tears welled up and sat stinging in her eyes. She covered her face with her dirty hands, and wondered what had become of Paulo and the Captain. If they had run into trouble, they would not be able to find her. What if they *never* found her? What if she never got home? Ever?

She took a deep breath in again and exhaled slowly through tight lips. She closed her eyes, and the tears that had been gathering there squeezed out and rolled freely down her cheeks.

"God," she whispered. "Please keep me safe. I know I haven't talked to you much... I know there's so much I don't understand... but all I want to understand now... is that You're with me..."

She suddenly thought about Jesus. These trembling hands, now wrapped tightly around her legs, were the same hands that had once cradled His tiny newborn form. Why had He gone to the trouble of becoming a baby? She was told it was so He could enter the depth of human struggle. This was one of the things she hadn't understood. Until now. She supposed Jesus must have felt alone many times, even scared...

In that thought, Evie felt comfort. Her racing heart slowed. The storm of restless nerves within her calmed. Maybe... they could be alone and scared together.

Although Evie suspected she was now outside the Sanctuary, she felt, inside this dark, dank, musty tree trunk with the bats and spiders and who-knows-what hunting her down outside, that she had just found a much greater Sanctuary.

HAZE OF THE PAST

||||||||||||||||||||||||||||||||||||||||||||||||||

"She'll fit right in," A1 was saying, as he and the Captain were watching the Sanctuary's latest arrival being placed in a hospital bed. "She'll feel all refreshed when she wakes up."

"She'll feel all confused," the Captain corrected.

"You're quite a negative person, aren't you?"

"Only when there's something to be negative about. What's going to happen to that woman after she wakes up?"

"She'll be taken to the Recovery Room for a little while to get her bearings, then sent to her new home. I'll have a chat with her in the next few days to welcome her and explain everything, and..."

"What about Evelyn? What about Paulo and probably hundreds of others who just stumbled in? They didn't ask for it. They didn't need your help. Why don't you let them go?"

A1 raised his thumb and forefinger up to his forehead. "Oh dear, dear, I *have* explained this to you already. *Everyone* needs my help. And by the way, I don't know names, only codes. It's much easier that way. I have a code for you too, of course. You're going to love it! From now on you are A7."

"Why such a low number? You have so many in your collection..."

"Well, since you're one of my special ones, I thought the least I could do was give you a more superior code. The code A7 used to belong to one of the early settlers, but he's... passed on since, and that means we can re-use the code."

"I'm not sure I like the idea of having a second-hand code."

"Oh, count it as an honour, dear chap. Come this way please." He started moving out of the room.

"What if I refuse?"

"You either cooperate... or you get the patch. I'm sure Z23 told you all about that."

The Captain shuddered.

"This way," A1 said again with a friendly smile. Always friendly. "I'll show you to your new home."

Paulo was looking for a way out, but he seemed to be in a maze of corridors. Just before the approaching voices caught up with him, he managed to quickly duck behind the corner of an adjacent hallway. He watched three men, dressed in white doctors' coats, pass him and then disappear around another corner.

Paulo rested his head back against the wall with a sigh of relief. Then out the corner of his eye, he saw some other white coats hanging on hooks along the wall next to him. He thought for a moment, took a big breath, and before he could change his mind, he lifted a coat off its hook and quickly put it on. He slid his arms in the sleeves, untucked the collar, tried to put on a bold, official expression, and scurried across the hallway to join the others.

The three men walking along became four men, now walking into an elevator. The others didn't seem to notice. They all carried on in their usual manner rather professionally as if they were expecting a fourth. When the lift stopped, Paulo felt a rush of butterflies, worrying what might be there when the doors opened.

When they did open, the butterflies were

suddenly great flapping bats and his blood throbbed inside his head when he saw, in front of him, a big, sumptuous office with a balding man in a suit standing there to greet him. He knew two things. One, that this must have been A1, and two, that this had been a very bad idea.

However, all the man said was: "Ah, there you are. Will you please show A7 the way out, get him some transport and send him straight to his new home. The details are here." He handed one of them a piece of paper.

Paulo's stomach lurched when A7 was brought forward. It was the Captain! He fought to keep his face still, willing no flicker of recognition to betray him. The Captain saw Paulo straight away, but *his* expression remained just as carefully unchanged.

"Thank you so much," A1 went on. "And be careful with him. He's a special case. Perhaps one of you could ride along with him. Make sure he gets there okay."

The four men escorted the Captain out of A1's office, through the main entrance and down the lush plant-lined pathway to the main road where a pastel-green and pink car was waiting.

"Why four of you?" the Captain stirred. "I'm not some raging animal."

"A1 said you're to be very well looked after,"

one of them said.

"Oh, how nice."

Paulo quickly took charge. "I'll go with him."

The others didn't argue. They handed Paulo the piece of paper, and moments later, he and the Captain were seated together in the back seat of the car, pulling away. They dared not speak yet. The driver had been given navigation directions, but who knew what other instructions he had if anything was amiss? They waited patiently in silence.

When the car stopped, they saw a small, tired, lonely looking house made of brick and stone with a corrugated tin roof. A thin wisp of smoke was wafting up out of a small chimney. Paulo headed straight for the wooden door and went inside quickly. The Captain, on the other hand, was stuck staring out the car window for a few moments.

With a gentle prompting from the driver, he exited the car without taking his eyes off the house. He walked slowly up the little path to the door, observing an old trough and wringer to his right, and a window box of flowers to his left at the house's only front window. Frowning, he cautiously followed Paulo inside, but he stopped again in the doorway, looking on at the room within.

"Captain," said Paulo. "I'm so glad to see you. How did you get in?"

The Captain was frozen. Stunned by a thousand electric nervous prickles stinging his gut, his throat, his heart. He slowly scanned every single detail of the room, speechless. His brow a tangle of furrows and his eyes like polished glass.

"Captain?" repeated Paulo. "Are you alright?"

The Captain observed an old splintery wooden table to his left, a few books resting on top with hand-made chairs around it. Beyond this, a small kitchen with the bare essentials; sink, oven, a larder.♣ To his right was a rug wearing thin under one single old-fashioned lounge chair, facing a simple fireplace. There was a small fire crackling inside. A wireless transistor radio sat perched on a battered, wooden side table next to the lounge chair.

"Captain?"

"How did they... know?" he muttered.

Paulo finally observed the room properly himself. "Is this... your home, Captain?"

"No," he quickly replied. "...Not anymore." He stepped closer to the table, placed a hand gently on the nearest chair, and stroked it slowly.

"It seems they've made copies of our living quarters back home," said Paulo. "To make us...

♣ A larder is a cabinet people would put food in that had to stay cool before we had refrigerators.

127

feel at home, I guess."

"What *is* home?" the Captain said as though he was a lightyear away, staring up at the rafters and at the few hanging pictures on the wall. "I suppose they... thought the Train was just transport. So they used this."

Paulo kept quiet. Not that he knew what to say anyway. It was clear the Captain needed room to sort through whatever was in his head.

"Mother sometimes read to us over there," he said, pointing to the corner with the rug and fireplace. "Before she..." he swallowed. "My brother and I would be on the carpet. Never sitting still, we were always... wrestling." He looked at the table. "I remember Aunt Ezzie helping me with my maths homework here..." A tiny smile crept onto his face. "She used to..."

"Yes, Captain?"

He blinked, returning from the deep haze of the past. He cleared his throat and said, "By Train."

"What?"

"We came in by Train. I decided to risk it after all."

"Are you okay, Captain? We can talk about this more if you want."

The Captain shook his head, staring at the carpet in the corner again for a few more seconds.

128

"We don't have time. And yes, I'm fine." He looked back at Paulo. "Are *you* alright?"

"Yes, fine! The last thing I remembered was when I was talking to you out on that green grass and stopping you from being pulled in and then the next thing, I was..."

"Waking up in a bed and then being taken to a Recovery Room?"

"Yes... Did that happen to you too?"

"No, but I saw it happen to someone else. A1 showed me. By the way, we saw you earlier. Roaming around the hallways of the Infirmary."

"No."

"Oh yes. But don't worry, we didn't see much. A1 was distracted by the new arrival."

"That's another strange thing. I was in the Infirmary, and when I came out from that lift, we were in a completely different..."

"You came out into A1's main office. The two buildings must be connected underground." While he was speaking, the Captain frowned a new frown and walked over to the kitchen area. He picked up a heavy box from a cupboard top. "What's this?"

"Looks a bit like a televiewer."

"Television, yes I know. But we never had one of these. And if we did, they didn't look like this."

"Maybe A1 wants everyone to have one."

The Captain put it down again.

"Perhaps we should see what's on it," said Paulo.

The Captain glanced back at Paulo, then pressed a power button. On came a cooking show with some bored looking chef showing viewers how to boil water. He changed the station.

"Oh R47 why did you have to do that? You know I love you already."

"But I always thought you wanted J22."

"J22 could never make me happy. It's you I love. No matter what 37F9 says."

He changed the station again.

"H18, I'm arresting you on suspicion of the murder of L411. Do you have anything to say?"

"I'm innocent Inspector 789! Believe me!"

He changed it again.

"Cleaning your teeth can be so stressful can't it! That's why you at home can have one of these top-of-the-range automatic teeth-cleaning..."

He changed it over again.

"Hello. My name is Sue. And isn't it another beautiful day! Here in the Sanctuary, we provide a stress-free environment. But sometimes, our minds wander back to the past. If this is you, here are a few hints on how to stay calm and relaxed."

The station was quickly changed again.

"...And in the latest news; a new arrival to the Sanctuary has found a happy ending in a new luxury two-bedroom unit. She's known as D14 and if you see her in town, be sure to say a friendly 'hello'. Also this week..."

"D14?" Paulo said out loud and confused. "That's not her."

The Captain recognised the newcomer as the young woman he saw on the screen in A1's office. "What's the problem?" he asked.

"It's not Evie!"

"Well of course it's not Evie. She wouldn't be a newcomer."

"But she was D14!"

Suddenly, the Captain's face became serious and very interested. He sat himself on a wooden dining chair and shuffled it close to the television, but by then, they'd moved on to different news. He frowned and straightened up, feeling both hope... and dread. "If there's now another D14," he said quietly, still staring at the screen, "then that means her code's being reused, and that means she's been replaced and *that* means..."

"What Captain?"

He looked straight at Paulo, wide-eyed. "She's no longer here. And she could be in terrible danger, in fact... we might already be too late."

CHAPTER

15

WHAT HAPPENED TO EVIE?

It was the Captain who had bolted out of the house first, leaving Paulo asking urgent questions.

"What do you plan to do, Captain?"

"I plan to ask A1 what happened to Evelyn."

"What, just like that? I don't want him to see me. He might capture me again and put me back in that waiting room."

"What waiting room?"

"People were waiting to have patches put on their arm. I got well away from there."

"Good boy."

"But... perhaps... instead of both of us, *you* should..."

"Whatever happens, we need to stay together."

They had sprinted right into the main part of the Sanctuary. They were heading straight for A1's office building, but a sudden voice blasted their plans apart, bringing them both to an abrupt stop.

"Getting some exercise?"

They turned around to see A1, sitting at a table outside a café, having a chilled glass of iced tea. "What a good idea! I suppose it's like you said A7, there's a time for everything. Resting," he pointed to his glass, "and activity." He pointed to them.

"We're not out for a Sunday jog," said the Captain indignantly, walking over to him. "We're out to find you actually."

"Oh, how delightful. What can I do for you?" A1 raised his hand forward, directing the Captain and Paulo to the seats opposite him. Two of them. Almost as though he had expected them.

The Captain eyed the chairs suspiciously, but then sat down and looked A1 straight in the eye. "What happened to Evelyn?"

"I'm sorry?"

"D14 then. Where is she?"

"I assume you mean the *previous* D14." He lowered his head and shook it gently. "She was a friend of yours I take it. I'm afraid there's been a terrible tragedy. You see, not long ago, she went for a swim. A deadly, man-eating fish was spotted...

and... she was never seen again."

"What?" Paulo said, without being able to control himself.

"Oh you," said A1. "I thought I recognised you earlier. You're A7's other friend. Well, you two might as well settle down here now. Make it your home. Let us take care of you. I know how awful it is to lose a friend. Naturally we'll have a proper funeral service for her. You won't be disappointed."

"Oh yes and who conducts that?" said Paulo, feeling a swell of anger rising up. "Sue? Mark? Or will it be Sue? Or perhaps Mark? Or any of the other mindless Marks and Sues you've got working here?"

"I don't believe you," the Captain said, taking no notice of Paulo's outburst. He hadn't taken his eyes off the smug, red-nosed man.

"I'm sorry?"

The Captain was as calm as a Sunday afternoon. "You want to know what I think happened? I think D14 finally found a way out of here. And because you'd never dream of broadcasting *that* on the news, you've made up some phoney story."

A1 lowered his eyes, looking melancholy. "I understand A7. We all have our own way of dealing with grief. But..."

The Captain just got up and left at that moment,

striding off without another word. Paulo followed right behind him.

"Well?" Paulo said after a short brisk walk. "Is it just wishful thinking or do you honestly disbelieve him?"

"Deception," said the Captain. "A1's built this whole place on it. So I don't have a single reason to believe anything he says."

Paulo uneasily started telling the Captain something he ought to have known. "The last time I saw Evie... something had happened to her. They'd given her a patch probably and she was just like all the others. In the state she was in... she'd never have tried to escape. What if she... did go for a swim..."

"Just stop there. We'll find her."

After a few minutes of trying to keep up with him, Paulo eventually realised that the Captain was heading towards the beach. "What are we doing, Captain?"

"Holding onto hopes and slim chances."

"That Evie's still alive?"

"Of course. I don't know where she is, but one thing I *do* know is that our Friend didn't allow her to be whisked away on my Train only to be killed by a shark or whatever it was. He must still have plans for her." He was searching for something in his pockets.

"Is that all you've got to go on?"

"Pretty much."

"And why are we heading to the sea?"

"The Train's parked there," the Captain said, pulling out his Train-driving goggles. "Logic dictates that if Evelyn's out, then we should get out too and re-join. Then come up with a plan to put a stop to all this Sanctuary nonsense."

Nonsense wasn't the word Paulo would have used. "A1's power here seems unstoppable."

"Unstoppable is a strong word. If the Train can get out as... *sort* of easily as it got in, then we have an advantage. As long as we can find... oh no."

"What is it?"

"Up ahead. In front of the Train."

"I can't see the Train."

"Just up ahead then. A1's got here before us."

It wasn't A1 personally. It was a group of four, burly men, dressed in black, waiting. Standing in a tight group between them and their way out.

The Captain kept walking slowly and casually, hoping that maybe they could trick them into thinking they were regular Sanctuary residents, out for a stroll along the beach. But as they moved, the men moved as well, blocking their path.

The Captain mumbled to Paulo, "Let's make a

run for it," and he took off like a bolt.

The Train was so close, it *just* seemed possible, but the men easily cut them off. The Captain was tackled from the side, tripped up off his feet and fell, stomach-down, on the ground. Paulo quickly tried to help him up, but one of the other men grabbed *him* and restrained him tightly around the ribcage. The Captain scrambled to his feet and found himself face to face with one of them. "Look, can we just talk about this like sensible, mature adults?"

Without warning, the man punched the Captain square in the jaw, sending him stumbling backwards in surprise, clutching his chin in pain. Before he'd had the chance to steady himself again, the man was there, ready to deliver a second blow. But with a sweep of his left arm, the Captain managed to block this one. And (even though there aren't many things the Captain hates more than violence), he had to fight back with a swing of his left arm. He landed his fist right in the man's stomach. The man coughed and wheezed a little and in his vulnerable position, the Captain then delivered a right-hook to his chin. The man staggered back, holding his face for a moment.

While this was happening, Paulo twisted and thrashed free and one of his legs unintentionally tripped the man up. The third man jumped into action, but Paulo used his new-found leg-tripping trick on him and sent *him* tumbling. This one rolled down a jagged, rocky slope towards the shoreline getting bruises and scratches all the way down. In that time, Paulo's first opponent had picked himself up off the ground and was coming for him again.

The Captain was just readying himself for defence again while *his* opponent and the fourth man came charging at him. Two against one. Out the corner of his eye, the Captain saw a long, white fold-out beach lounge and in a flash, he turned, picked it up and held it in front of his body like a shield. It was much heavier than he'd expected and when both men rammed into it, they coiled back in pain. Only one of them was able to recover from such a collision, and he looked straight into the Captain's eyes menacingly.

Paulo found the Captain and positioned himself against his back so they could defend from both sides. His opponent was coming at him with a strong, clenched fist. The Captain's opponent raised up a strong arm, snatched the beach lounge from him and threw it to the ground. Both men were ready to deliver their mightiest blow. And at the last second, the Captain and Paulo both ducked down to dodge...

...And they heard a loud thud above them.

When they opened their eyes, they saw their opponents both lying, knocked out on the sandy ground. They looked at each other and then breathed out in relief, the Captain not exactly feeling proud that they'd just injured four men. He rolled up the sleeve of the one lying next to him and found a patch stuck to his bicep. He peeled it off carefully and examined it. Just a square bit of clear, blueygreen plastic.

Then, as the two of them started to stand up, there was a rustling, scuttling noise nearby. Paulo saw something move out the corner of his eye. "Did that bush just move?"

(There was an eruption of laughter in A1's office at that moment. A1 was seated in his big chair, leaning back comfortably, staring up at the big screen on his wall as if watching a good movie on telly.)

"What?" said the Captain.

"I swear that bush behind us just moved."

At that moment, there were five or so dry, prickly tumble weeds rolling towards them, gathering at their feet.

"What on Serothia?" Paulo uttered, before one of them tumbled onto his foot, and started climbing up his leg. "Ergh!" he exclaimed. "Get it off!"

But the Captain was busy with his own tumble weeds to worry about. There were now at least ten of them all ganging up around them, rolling onto them and climbing up their bodies. If they tried to move, they were painfully jabbed on every side by the prickles, which were rapidly growing into thorns. They were cut off again from their route to the Train, immobilised.

(A1 was enjoying the entertainment immensely. "Oh, this is the funniest thing I've seen in ages! *Did that bush just move.* Ha ha! Very good!")

"Can you stop them, Captain?"

"Er..." The Captain tried to get his hands inside his pockets but the sharp, entwining thorns were threatening to pierce him. "Not really, no. Ow!"

A1 sighed and finally stood up. "Well, I suppose I'd better go and get them out of their little pickle." He turned off the big screen and the wall came gliding back to conceal it again. "Or *prickle* in this case," he said on his way out with a chuckle.

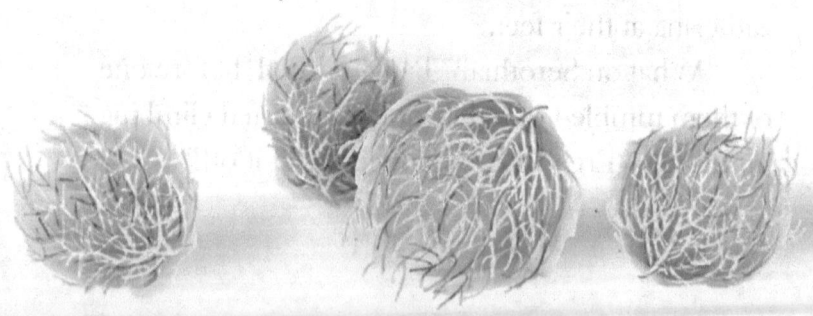

A sharp dagger of sunlight came streaming in through the opening of the tree trunk and woke Evie. Her mouth was dry and her feet were two blocks of ice. She took a few moments to compose herself before cautiously peeping her head out into the sunlight. There appeared to be no danger now. Whatever had been pursuing her last night had obviously given up or found some easier prey. She climbed out, brushed herself off and tried to comb her fingers through her hair, before they got stuck in all the knots. She looked at the dense forest all around her, with no clue what to do next.

"God?" she said feebly. "Can you hear me? Can... can you see me? What should I do?" She was standing there for about half a minute, getting no reply. *Why can't God just use one of those big, booming voices and say something clearly like how everyone imagines it happened in the Bible?*

Soon however, there did come a sound. Not a big, booming voice but a small, pretty one. It was a bird. The most beautiful bird-song Evie had ever heard. She instinctively looked up to the trees to try and find the bird responsible. For some reason, she expected a more fancy, colourful bird, but when she found it on a branch nearby, it was just brown with a few dull yellow speckles. It opened its beak, and out trickled that sweet song again. It sounded like a tiny flute made of glistening sunshine.

Evie crept quietly toward it to get a closer look. Amongst all the danger and confusion of the last day, a smile finally made its way to her lips. She dared to take one more step, but it was a mistake. Her foot broke through some loose bracken on the forest floor. The ground gave way beneath her. She gasped. The bird flew away, and she was falling.

CHAPTER

16

SANCTUARY UNDERGROUND

|||||||||||||||||||||||||||||||||||||||||||||||||||||

A series of hard concrete steps rushed up and smacked into Evie's body one after the other. "Oof! Ow!" She sat up and saw at the top of the steps was some sort of trap door or cellar door that she'd crashed through, covered over by overgrown vines and mouldy leaves. Apart from the dappled sunlight dripping through from the opening above, the place where she'd landed was in darkness. She stood, brushed herself off, and, as always, let her curiosity pull her a few steps deeper into the blackness.

She hadn't roamed far when a dull pool of light appeared, hovering over a small spot of the concrete floor ahead. Evie's stomach lurched. Someone was sitting there, legs crossed on an old mattress. Alone.

Facing away from her. Evie stepped silently closer and plucked up the courage to say a feeble, "Hello?"

The figure did not move, as if it... *she* hadn't heard her. It was a girl. One step closer enabled Evie to recognise the side of her face. "Laura!" she yelled out. But still, it seemed Laura couldn't hear her. It was only when Evie came and stood right in front of her that Laura's face lit up. She stood to her feet and spoke, but no sound came out. It was like a weird dream. Evie was no lip-reader, but she could tell Laura was trying to say her name, and after that, it looked like *help me.*

Then when Laura raised her hands and they appeared to press up against an invisible wall, Evie realised she *was* talking, probably at the top of her voice, but Evie just couldn't hear her. There was an invisible, sound-proof barrier between them.

Evie noticed that next to the mattress, there was also a small flask of water, an empty bowl, and a small but deep basin thing, which she realised, with horror, was a toilet.

Laura started saying more than just 'help me'.

Evie shook her head. "What? *What?* I can't... What are you saying?"

Laura then gave up using her mouth to speak and started making gestures. She pointed at something above her and then wiggled her finger in a way you might do to depict a worm. She mouthed a word with it in an exaggerated way.

Wheel, it looked like, or *witch? Why would she be saying witch?* "Did a witch put you in here?" Evie said. "No, that's silly."

She watched as Laura then held up one hand vertically and first used the index finger on the other hand to prod her palm, and then used her finger and thumb to... draw on her palm? No... peel skin? No... Evie watched her mouth carefully. She then suddenly realised. *Switch!*

What switch? Evie looked all over the place for one. Then she remembered where Laura had been pointing and she stood up and felt with her hands along the wall of the invisible box. Right up the top in the shadows, which was far above head height for Evie, was a switch. She flicked it, and Laura came somersaulting out of the little box.

"Evie I don't know what to say," said Laura with a tired smile. "How did you find me?"

"I don't know really. I kind of just... stumbled down here... literally."

"I was told no one would ever find me."

"Well they lied obviously," Evie smiled. "What are you doing down here?"

"It's my new home sweet home."

"Doesn't look very sweet to me," Evie said, grimacing at the toilet.

"You're kidding right? You think I chose to come down here?"

"I don't understand."

"I'll have to explain later."

"Well, the opening's just over there, let's go!"

"We can't. Not yet."

"Why not?"

Laura, in reply, walked past Evie and to another wall by the entrance. She seemed to know exactly where to go to find another collection of buttons and switches, even though they were all in darkness. She flicked one and said, "See for yourself."

Dozens upon dozens of dull lights faded to life, stretching in endless rows that receded into the depths of an underground warehouse. Underneath each light, Evie could now see, was a person in the exact same predicament as Laura had been in, moments ago. Each in their individual tiny invisible soundproof box with their own little mattress and their own little toilet.

Evie was speechless for a moment. All she could utter was, "Whoa." Then she managed to ask, "How did you know about those controls?"

"Because they come down here sometimes to

feed us... I'm right by the entrance. And I always paid attention to what they were doing."

"And you're all just left down here in the dark? Are all these people from the Sanctuary?"

Laura nodded. "When people become too hard for A1 to control, they 'die' up there, and 'live' down here. A1 still owns us but we're out of the way so we don't cause any more trouble. He works so hard up there to make you comfortable and happy, like you're in your own home. Down here, we're just kept like animals in a cage."

"How *does* A1 know exactly what all our homes look like?"

Laura shrugged. "I figured they might be scanning people's memories or something when they first arrive. He thinks it would make us feel more comfortable here, but it's just the opposite don't you think?"

Evie nodded glumly again, staring unseeingly at all the people in the boxes. "We have to do something," she whispered. "But what?"

"Well," Laura said quietly. "I may have a plan. But first I need to find it."

"You need to *find* your plan?"

CHAPTER

17

INTRODUCING MR CAMERON

||||||||||||||||||||||||||||||||||||||||||||||||||||

Laura had darted into the disturbing museum of glass boxes, and Evie was quite happy to stay and wait for her. It wasn't long until Laura emerged again, but she hadn't come out alone. A tall, ageing, tired looking man was with her.

"This," said Laura, almost out of breath, "is my idea." Then she turned and looked up at the man. "I'm sorry, I don't even know your name."

"Cameron," he said in a tired, but friendly voice. "Ben Cameron."

Laura looked back at Evie. "Mr. Cameron's Sanctuary code was A7, and you know what that means."

Evie started to shake her head, but then an idea

flashed into her mind. "He was the seventh person to live in the Sanctuary?"

"Seventh person registered, yeah. He was there when it all started. If anyone knows the ins and outs of the Sanctuary, it'd be him! Right?" The last word was aimed at Mr. Cameron.

"Well, I know its foundations, its layout, its original purpose, the network, that sort of thing," said Mr. Cameron. He had an English accent, like A1.

"But, how come you're down here?" Evie asked. "As one of A1's trapped animals? What happened?"

"I was part of a council," he wrenched out a violent cough. "There were eight of us. A1, the head of course. We were the head of staff for a luxury holiday resort establishment called *The Sanctuary*. As the years went by, A1 was... changing. He was becoming twisted in his ideas about what the place should be. What it should be for. He made it so we didn't have names anymore but codes, and then he included the customers and soon, he didn't want to let people go." He coughed again. "Eventually the rest of the council had to take a stand. Old Cartwright and Filby passed away shortly after that. The others... actually stuck by A1's side, remaining members of his staff. They're probably still up there working for him now. I couldn't understand how they could go along with what A1 was doing. Perhaps they were just frightened of him. Or hungry for wealth, perhaps A1 offered them huge salaries. But I couldn't stand by and let it all happen. I knew how he planned to keep people here. I knew what he was doing to people who wouldn't cooperate. I did all I could to convince him it was wrong... and pointless, I mean, what does he gain from it? Just that it... satisfies him. To collect people. An odd sort of obsession." He finished by coughing again.

Laura patted him on the back and stabled him. "Do you want to sit down?"

Mr Cameron refused, saying that he'd been doing nothing but sitting all the time in that horrible box. "In the end I was too much of a threat to his plans, and so he faked my death and sent me down here through some teleport device thing that he'd created. Goodness knows what other frightful things he's created to serve his purposes while I've been down here."

"It was only by chance that I found out you existed down here, Mr. Cameron," said Laura. "When they came down here with one of the meals, they brought you out to talk with you. And because they have to open the barriers enough to push some food through, I overheard enough to give me some hope that you might be able to help us defeat A1."

"Defeat A1?" Mr. Cameron said, his tone of voice utterly dashing all hopes that were welling up inside Laura and Evie.

"Well, please tell me... that with your knowledge of this place, we could possibly have a chance at stopping him."

A faint smile crept onto Mr. Cameron's lips. "Oh, I believe we might have a chance. It was just the way you put it. *Defeat A1...* sounds like some kind of computer game."

The girls sighed in hopeful relief.

"I know there's got to be a way," said Laura. "But then on top of it all, we've somehow got to find a way of getting home and fixing our lives up."

"Getting home's the easy part," Evie said, thinking of the Train. (That is, if she would ever see it and the Captain again.) "But I can't imagine how we're going to stop A1."

"I'm sure if we knock our heads together and be smart about it," said Mr Cameron, "we can come up with something."

"Knock our heads together? Is that really necessary?" said Evie.

"That's an expression, young lady."

"Oh," Evie's cheeks flushed. "I knew that."

"But before we do anything," said Laura, "we

need to know how to get *out* of the Sanctuary, so that we know we have an escape-route when we need it."

"Oh!" Evie exclaimed.

"What's wrong?"

"Nothing! But I just didn't realise until now that you wouldn't know!"

"Know what?"

"Well, I'm not one hundred percent sure... but maybe like, ninety-eight percent sure... that we're actually already outside the Sanctuary."

Laura's eyes grew wide and twinkled with rapidly rising hopes. "Hold up, ninety-eight percent? What does that ninety-eight percent rest on?"

Evie bit her lip. "...A feeling. But a very strong one!"

"Or do you mean the absence of a feeling?" Mr. Cameron asked.

Evie locked eyes with him. "Yeah! And I reckon if we just go up those steps, you'll see what I mean."

"What about all these people?" said Laura.

"Let's accomplish our mission," said Mr Cameron with calm optimism, "and then we can easily free them all."

The girls smiled at him. And moments later,

they were walking through the forest above.

"Wow," Laura said. "A real deep, dark forest."

"Exactly," said Mr. Cameron. "Not like the manufactured forests in the Sanctuary." He breathed in a long, deep breath of fresh air. "You're right, Evie. I do believe we're not in the Sanctuary anymore."

"Yeah but... wait," said Laura. "We need to start off *inside* the Sanctuary don't we? If we're going to confront A1."

Evie rolled her eyes around, feeling just a tad pleased with herself that she had the answer to this one too. "Well... if we're outside the Sanctuary now... then I know a way back in. If you'll just follow me." And she led the way, leaving the other two guessing at her every move. She felt (with a little giggle to herself) a teensy-weensy bit like the Captain.

CHAPTER

18

A JUMP TO THE HEARTBEAT

Evie was striding quickly and determinedly back through the thick forest. "Where is it?" she said to herself. "It can't be too far from here..."

The other two were struggling to keep the pace because Laura had to keep waiting for Mr. Cameron to catch up every ten or so steps.

"We passed my tree earlier and I wasn't running all that far from that animal," continued Evie.

"Animal?" said Laura worriedly. "There's animals out here?"

"Hey, this looks familiar," Evie said, coming to a stop.

When Mr. Cameron reached them, he said

breathlessly, "It certainly does look familiar."

"You recognise this place?" asked Evie.

He spoke between gasps for breath. "If I'm not mistaken... then I not only recognise it... I helped design it."

"You designed a forest?" asked Laura. "But it looks so... natural."

"No, no. I helped design..."

"The portal?" asked Evie.

"Yes. I gather... that was how you... came to be here, young Evie."

Evie nodded.

"It was created... er, to be an emergency exit."

"An emergency exit?" asked Laura, hardly believing it.

"Yes. And the *only* exit now, since... A1 seems to have... dismantled what used to be... the main entrance. People were originally *supposed* to be able to leave, you know. It's basically... a doorway to another dimension. A dimension... er, where the Sanctuary lies. And er... ah, there's a familiar tree."

"That's it!" shouted Evie.

They all arrived and stopped in front of the tree with the big hole in its trunk, and they hesitated there for a moment.

Nervously, Laura said, "Well come on. What are we waiting for?"

"It's the thought of stepping back into the Sanctuary," said Evie with unease. "Why *is* it in another dimension?"

"Well, like any holiday," said Mr. Cameron, "you want to feel like you're cut off from the rest of the world. This way, you really *were* in a sense." He took a few more moments to get his breath back, and then he said, making a move towards the tree, "Come on. Give me a boost, will you?"

"Into the tree?" said Laura.

"You'll see in a tick," said Evie.

They helped the fragile Mr. Cameron up into the hole in the tree. He put one leg in first, so that he was straddling the trunk, then he ducked his head through, and the rest of his body disappeared into the black. The two girls followed, and Laura was amazed to suddenly find herself popping up out of the ground and having to climb up onto land.

Mr. Cameron was on his tummy from the climb through and the girls helped him up.

"This forest looks so different," Laura said. "What a bummer I never found this portal myself."

"Now," said Mr Cameron, "here, in the Sanctuary, we're technically dead so unless we draw attention to ourselves, we should be able to get around unnoticed. Try and blend in, but remember, A1 knows the truth. That we're *not* dead, and there's hidden cameras nearly everywhere."

"So where do we go?" asked Laura.

"We must risk going to the town centre," said Mr. Cameron. "We'll try and come up with a plan on the way for how to take A1 by surprise."

The three of them looked for the quickest way out of the forest and straight into the heartbeat of the Sanctuary.

The heartbeat of course, was where all the life of the Sanctuary flowed from. The control centre. The main building where A1's office was. And it wasn't long until Mr Cameron, Evie and Laura were nearby. They sat themselves down at a table outside the café, and soon they had tropical drinks in front of them with tiny umbrellas sticking out the top.

"Well, that's it there," Mr Cameron said in a hushed voice, pointing to the big, round, concrete building beyond the high fences. "That's where A1 lives, where he works, and where he takes a holiday. All the controls for the Sanctuary are in there."

"I wondered what that big ugly building was," said Evie.

"You never went in there?" asked Laura.

"Nup. What's it like?"

Laura shrugged. "Just as dull as the Infirmary. They're more or less the same building."

"Huh?"

"They connect, underground," explained Mr Cameron.

"Well it's very impressive," said Evie, "but how do we get in? Look at those huge gates! And the cameras all around!"

"Well I don't know, but there's a chance the security code at the gate will still be the same as it was when I was working here. All the council members knew it."

"It's a pretty slim chance, isn't it?" Laura said, doubtfully.

Mr. Cameron gave a serious nod of the head. "Very slim indeed."

CHAPTER

19

AT THE CONTROLS

I don't know if you've ever been covered head to toe with prickle bush, but let me tell you, it's not a pleasant experience, as I'm sure you can imagine.

Paulo wriggled and squirmed, but the prickles only gripped him tighter. He knew the Captain was still beside him, and he remembered one of the gadgets the Captain owned. "I know you always look for just the right moment, Captain, but... do you think maybe now might be a good time to use your Atom Relocating Molecular Teleport Device?"*

"I think you could have hit the nail on the head there, young friend. If I could just..." The Captain

---

* One must think very carefully before using an Atom Relocating Molecular Teleport Device because once used (just once), it takes twenty-four hours to fully charge up before it's ready to be used again.

tried getting inside his pocket, but several prickles were clamping down hard on his hand and wrist as though they knew what he was trying to do. "Ahhh!" A large thorn tore his skin as he pushed his hand further down to his pocket.

At that moment, A1 arrived at the beach and was walking towards the big pathetic mass of wriggling prickles. Although now, they were less like prickles and more like growing, stabbing, fat daggers.

The Captain pushed past the pain and let the thorn tear through his skin so that he could reach into his pocket. Another thorn pushed into his forearm. The dry, barbed vines were tightening on him. But his hand was inside his pocket.

A1 stopped when he had reached the big hunk of thorn bush on the beach.

The Captain reached his other hand out, getting more deep scratches, and grabbed Paulo's arm.

A1 took a brief moment to laugh out loud at the sight. Then he ordered the bushes off of them, and at his command, they tumbled clumsily away.

A1's face changed. His smile twisted, scrunched, and then vanished. "WHERE ARE THEY?" he roared, causing the little prickle bushes to shrink further away into the undergrowth. A1 searched angrily in every nook and cranny along the beach. The Train, of course, he couldn't see, and not being able to see it, (because it was invisible to him and he couldn't see it) he walked straight into the side of it. And because he wasn't just walking, but walking with such a fiery, tempestuous rage, he knocked himself out. As luck would have it (even though that is a terrible thing to say) he got a good deal of solid sleep for the next little while.

The Captain and Paulo materialised in a new place and they both tumbled onto the floor. They got up straight away, giving their limbs a stretch and scratching all the itches they had from the prickles. The Captain examined the back of his hand. Blood was seeping out and dripping onto the floor. He looked for something to wrap it up in.

Paulo looked around, confused. "Why didn't you materialise us inside the Train? That's where we were trying to get to before we were attacked by A1's thugs and prickle bushes."

"I know, but that was before we were attacked by A1's thugs and prickle bushes."

"Huh?"

They were right smack in the middle of A1's office, and after settling for the handkerchief in his pocket to wrap around his hand, the Captain didn't waste any more time. He strode over to a wall, pressed the button that he remembered A1 had pressed, and part of the wall slid back to reveal the big screen. Without the Captain having to do anything else, it displayed the scene of the beach where they had just been seconds before. They saw A1 there, the red of his bulging nose spreading to the rest of his face as he searched the beach.

"A1's down there to collect us," said the Captain.

"Yes but now he's discovered we're not there, he might come straight back here."

"He may well, so we don't have long."

They heard the *thump* suddenly and looked up at the screen.

"Oooh," said the Captain, cringing. "Nasty."

"Did you plan that?"

"Of course not. I can't help it if he doesn't watch where he's walking."

"But that's the Train he walked into. He probably *was* watching where he was going."

The Captain realised he still had his goggles on. "Oh, whoops. I forget sometimes." He removed them and tucked them inside a pocket.

"Well now that we're here, what shall we do?"

"Have a general snoop about, was my plan."

The Captain went straight to A1's desk. From the front, it just looked like a simple large, white, polished desk. It curved around to form almost a semi-circle of desk, as though it was engulfing the chair behind it in a kind of air-hug. When the Captain walked around behind the desk, he saw drawers and drawers and drawers. Big wide, deep ones, five across and three down. He opened one of the top ones and it slid out smoothly and silently.

Now I don't know about you, but I find drawers interesting. Especially other people's drawers, if you ever get the chance to look in one without them catching you. Sometimes I think someone's drawer (or more accurately what's *in* the drawer) can tell you what kind of person they are. In light of this, I think you'll find the contents of A1's drawer quite interesting, as did the Captain.

As the controlling type of person we know A1 to be, what would you expect to find in his drawers?

Controls of course! There were buttons and levers, knobs and switches. Lights and microphones, toggles and speakers. The Captain began to understand how A1 seemed to have eyes and ears everywhere in the Sanctuary, how he could know everything that was going on. One drawer was for audio communication to and from the Infirmary. In another drawer, you could choose between listening to the sounds of the village square and main streets, a restaurant kitchen, or a person's living room. A number of drawers were dedicated to surveillance. There were rows of buttons all labelled: 'Sanctuary Café', 'Sanctuary Newsagent', 'Village Square: East", 'Village Square: North' and so on. One of the labels said 'Infirmary', under which was 'Halls', 'Beds', 'Waiting Rooms', 'Recovery Room', 'Patching Room' and so on. When the buttons were pressed, up on the big screen would appear live views of all these places instantly.

In another drawer there were buttons labelled: 'External Consulting Rooms'. All of these looked like ordinary therapy rooms where people go to receive counselling and psychiatric care. Nearby, there were two buttons labelled 'receive' and 'release' (whatever that meant) and underneath, buttons that turned out to be for the surveillance of the land just outside the Sanctuary, in the other dimension. The Captain was about to try another button to see what would come up next, when suddenly there was some activity on the screen. There was another one of those wanderers out in the open field. He was alone, walking around, enjoying the fresh air and the warm sunshine. Perhaps he was one of those people Asher had rounded up out there.

Suddenly, the man was engulfed by a blinding light. At the same moment, a computerised voice said, *"Attention needed of Sanctuary Resident A1. Potential Sanctuary visitor at outer-dimensional field held in time suspension zone. Please choose 'receive' or 'release'."*

The Captain looked down at the buttons. *Receive. Or Release.* The Captain looked up at the man caught in the time suspension zone, then he looked back down at the buttons again. He shrugged and pressed *Release.* The voice said: *"Are you sure? If so, press 'release'. If you made a mistake, press 'receive'."*

He pressed *Release.*

"Are you sure?"

"Yes," he pressed it again.

"Are you sure you want to complete this action?"

"Yes!" he replied pressing it again.

That was the last time the voice spoke. He quickly looked back up to the screen. The light had melted away from the man and he blinked, shook his head and kept on walking.

Why does he even have a 'release' button? thought the Captain.

The two travellers looked at each other, looked

165

back at the screen, and then back at each other again. Paulo let off an amazed one-syllable laugh, and the Captain sat down on A1's chair staring over all the controls in the open drawers. Almost in disbelief, the Captain said, "It's just like running a computer. The Sanctuary depends on the person who's controlling it."

"That seems obvious doesn't it?"

"But it's not like the operation is set in motion and impossible to stop. The Sanctuary's just a giant computer that needs someone to tell it what to do."

Paulo looked blank.

"Don't you see what this means?" The Captain sunk back comfortably in the chair. His voice darkened. "I have the power." He joined the fingertips of his right hand to the fingertips of his left hand. "I have thousands of people under my control while I sit in this chair. There is no free will. There is only *my* will because I have their strings wrapped around my fingers and *nothing* these people do will be outside my control." He lowered his hands slowly and ran them gently over all the controls in front of him. "I could rule the world with this power. I could rise up as the most feared being in the entire galaxy and slowly gain control of it, star system by star system. Today the Sanctuary... tomorrow... *the universe!!*"

Paulo was frowning worriedly. "Are you sure that's what it means, Captain?"

He suddenly spoke in his normal voice and looked at Paulo like a friend again. "Well the point is it could mean that for someone but for us it means we could actually stop A1. And it's going to be much simpler than I thought."

"There's no button anywhere that says *release everybody from the Sanctuary* is there?" said Paulo.

"Unfortunately not."

"How about *Take all power away from A1?*"

"Uh-uh. Ooh, have a look at this," said the Captain, after pressing one of the buttons in the 'External Consulting Rooms' drawer.

They could see a consulting room with a female consultant bringing a client into the small adjoining room. Soon after, there was another alert.

Attention needed of Sanctuary Resident A1.

167

Potential Sanctuary visitor in Forgetting Room. Transition to Sanctuary confirmation needed. Please choose 'receive' or 'reject'.

"Reject it! Reject it!" said Paulo.

"I was going to," said the Captain. With a smile and a lick of his lips, he pressed the button that was labelled *'reject'*. After several questions asking whether he was sure he absolutely wanted to do this action, the client was released by *Sue* and by the looks of it, was allowed to go home.

They laughed and then the Captain came across another section of the control panel labelled 'Sue and Mark control bank'. He pressed a button, and up came the words *'ARE YOU SURE YOU WANT TO SHUT DOWN THIS 'SUE' UNIT?'*

"They're just bots," said the Captain. He pressed *'yes'* and the *Sue* on the screen froze in place, like she'd been simply switched off.

They laughed again in astonishment.

"Having fun?" said a voice from the doorway. It wasn't Paulo's. It wasn't the Captain's. It didn't even belong to the tiny imp that lived inside the Captain's breast pocket. It was A1, and he was standing just inside the room with a tough, muscly person dressed in black at either side of him.

"Er, yes actually," replied the Captain, taking a small bottle of some kind of juicy drink out of his pocket and having a sip.

"We should have kept an eye on the beach, Captain," Paulo said, sidling across the room to stand next to the Captain.

"Yes, well I didn't know how to get the picture-in-picture mode," he muttered back.

"I'm sure I don't have to remind you that this is my private office," said A1, slowly and calmly moving further into the room.

"No no no, of course not. I was actually just admiring this desk of yours. All these controls!" The Captain pushed drawers in and pulled drawers out and pressed a few buttons while he was talking. "May I just say, what an amazing set up you've got here." Just then, the Captain stopped pressing buttons as he shot a passing glance at that big screen in the wall. It felt as if his heart and lungs had vaulted skyward but he kept his face unchanged. Paulo saw it too. It was Evie on the screen, in the main square of the Sanctuary with two other people, sitting at a café table, trying not to be noticed.

He quickly pushed another button to get the screen to display something else. "It's all rather impressive but to put it plainly I think you could make a few improvements." Just then, something else came up on the screen at the press of another button, that grabbed the Captain's curiosity.

"Oh really?" A1 replied. "Well to put it *plainly* for you, A7... I'm not really interested."

"What's this?" the Captain asked with a frown, looking at the big screen.

A1 looked. He momentarily seemed a little worried, but then he relaxed into a calm, sly smile.

The view on the screen was dull and dismal. Little pools of dim light, sad individuals crouched alone..."

"The Sanctuary Underground," A1 replied watching the reaction in the Captain's face carefully. "It's part of my collection."

The Captain didn't need any further explanation. In that moment, a whole new, terrifying reality was made clear to him.

"I don't know how you got out of my disguised restraining units," A1 said calmly. "but you are beginning to make me quite angry."

"Oh really?" said the Captain with flared nostrils, but he refused to be distracted by his own growing anger. "Well, I *am* pleased. That's just what I was going for. You see because, not only does anger make people dangerous, it can make them a little bit careless as well, did you know that?"

With a huge, amused smile, A1 replied, "No I didn't know that. But tell me A7, who were you suggesting was the careless one?"

Just then, both the Captain and Paulo felt something being stuck down onto their wrists. Two men dressed in black had crept up behind them and now Paulo's eye-lids drooped. He swooned and fell into the waiting arms of one of the men. A second or so later, the Captain, seeing the patch on his wrist said, "Ah, me I suppose." Then he too swayed woozily, and collapsed.

CHAPTER

HANDY SOLUTIONS

The Captain was waiting with his eyes closed, lying on a metal trolley bed. He had heard wheels squeaking and gliding over the smooth floor, the sound of an elevator, and doors opening and closing. When all was silent, and he sensed they were alone, he opened his eyes and looked around. He saw Paulo, unconscious, on another trolley bed beside him. They were in a round, clinical room. Some kind of laboratory. *Just as well I brought my Temporary Toxin Neutralising Solution from the Train,* he thought. *Useful thing to have.*

He climbed off the bed, took the patch off his arm and crinkled it up to throw away. He leant over

Paulo, checked his pulse, and gently lifted his eyelids. *As I thought. The boy with kaleidoscope eyes. Powerful stuff, these patches. Luckily not as powerful as my neutralising solution. Looks like just a sleeping-aid thankfully.*

Aren't you going to take it off?

It'll probably wake him.

Isn't that the idea?

No harm in leaving him there for a bit to rest.

The Captain started laughing softly and shaking his head. *Look at this place! Why would they leave us in here?*

I presume because they think you're asleep.

I can do some damage in here. Now, let me see, what do we have?

He rubbed his hands together, eyes shining, and noticed a cabinet with boxes of patches all stacked up and ready to use. Beside them were rows and rows of tubs, labelled with different symbols. The Captain considered destroying the contents of the whole cabinet, but he knew this couldn't be their whole supply.

Then he saw a fire extinguisher behind the

door.♣ He could start a fire with his Manuel Hand
Operating Fuel-Injected Flame Combustion
Apparatus. It would create a distraction, the place
might even be evacuated. But in the Captain's
experience, fire was a dangerous ally. One moment
it can be on your side, but in a flash, turn against
you. The Captain was still waiting for the right plan.
The one that was the quickest, the safest and the
surest way of doing the job.

He rested for a bit, slumping against the wall
and giving his neck a rub. No plans were coming.
He had a moment of advantage in this room, but he
was coming up blank. He sighed, feeling a little out
of steam. He closed his eyes, but he wasn't trying to
have a power nap. He was waiting. And just then,
there was commotion outside and he had to think
quick. He could either lie back down and pretend
to be asleep still, or...

There was a rack near the door with doctor's
coats hanging on it.♦ He rushed over and put one
on, feeling a sudden rush of hot fury when his arm
wouldn't go through one of the arm holes because
the person before him hadn't put it completely back
through the right way.

♣ As all workplaces must have one or several as an Occupational Health
and Safety regulation. Yes, even on other planets.

♦ Great minds think alike, I guess.

The voices were right outside the door, and just in time, the Captain, in his white coat and last-minute addition of a pair of glasses he had in his pocket, stood at the head of Paulo's bed appearing as though he was performing a check-up on him.

Two female nurses stopped in the doorway.

"Come in, come in," said the Captain. "You're not interrupting anything. Just making sure this one's not going to wake up for a while."

They stepped in further. One of them said, "There's a top-up scheduled for now. Is the lab free?"

"Yes, yes! By all means."

The nurses came in, followed by a line of men and women dressed in black. The Captain frowned in curiosity and wheeled Paulo out of the way.

"What exactly are you doing?" he asked carefully.

"We told you, a top-up," one of them replied. "We've got to give these workers another fresh patch. They don't all work for A1 of their own free will, remember?"

"Yes, of course, well... er let me help you."

"That would be good actually. Sometimes I feel a bit nervous with all these strong muscly people, close to top-up time."

"I'll stay, if it makes you feel safer. You two start

175

getting them ready, I'll get the patches." The Captain didn't know exactly what he was going to do yet, but he could feel it. About to reveal itself. Opportunity.

"Don't forget to wash your hands before and after," one of the nurses said. "This is the solution we need here." She pointed to one particular tub.

"And the gloves are there," said the other one.

Thank you, thought the Captain. *I just got the idea I was waiting for!*

He was in charge of soaking the patches in the very solution that causes temporary loss of self-control and free-will. He went over to the bench and while always keeping one eye on those nurses, he removed the necessary amount of patches from the boxes and carried them and the tub of solution over to the sink. He also found a similar tub which was empty and carried that over as well.

He ran the water in the sink to wash his hands, holding the identical tub underneath the tap, filling it up. Instead of soaking the patches in the solution, he soaked them, bold as anything, in the tub of plain water. He stretched on some rubbery gloves, being careful not to disturb the handkerchief tied over his wound. The nurses didn't so much as glance over, which was good, for obvious reasons.

"Now ladies," said the Captain, "a quick test for you. How long must you soak the patches for?"

One of them replied immediately, "Between two and three minutes."

This is too easy, thought the Captain. "Very good," he said. When he'd waited a little longer than two minutes, he took them out one by one and handed them to one of the nurses, and from then, it was like a well-rehearsed production line. The Captain would hand a patch to the first nurse, she would place it on the upper arm of a groggy worker, then the other nurse would take him or her to a different room connected to the lab a little way off that looked like a sick bay. The Captain was just trying to get a subtle closer look at this adjoining room, when one of the nurses said:

"These haven't been soaked long enough."

He was a little startled when he turned and saw the nurse looking right at him.

"Between two and three minutes," he replied. "By the book."

"But they're not green in colour."

The Captain uncontrollably *gulped. Not so easy perhaps...* "Did... didn't you know?"

"Know what?"

"The new solution A1's been trialling. We began using them today. Looks less obvious on the arm."

After a short pause to think, the nurses seemed to accept it. After all, *he* was the doctor.

The Captain kept breathing evenly, keeping one eye on Paulo. By the end of the procession, there were about fifteen or twenty workers all sitting in the sick bay. The nurses thanked him politely and left him to look after his 'patient'. This time of course, the door was not locked – the nurses had been innocent traitors.

When he was sure they were gone, the Captain decided it was time to wake Paulo up, before *their* nurses or doctors came to 'look after' *them*.

CHAPTER

21

THE BATTLE OF THE CAPTIVES

|||||||||||||||||||||||||||||||||||||||||||

Paulo was finally able to stand on his own two feet by himself again, but he needed a prod in the side from the Captain every ten seconds to wake him up again.

"What happened, Captain?" Paulo said groggily.

"We were drugged with a patch. Well, you were. Just a sleeping one."

"What are we going to do?"

"I have a part of a plan brewing. Not sure where it's going yet." The Captain peered out the door to keep an eye on the corridor. "Perhaps if you tell me more about what you've seen of this place. When you were snooping around in the Infirmary. Did you learn anything?" ...He looked back at Paulo. He'd fallen asleep again, sliding down the wall. "Paulo," he said, gently tugging him up. He had to ask his question again.

Paulo rubbed his head and yawned. "Er... there was just a bunch of weird classes going on..."

"Classes? What sort of cl..."

They heard footsteps out in the corridor. The Captain froze and straightened his back against the inside of the door, listening, searching the room and his mind for more ideas.

He looked at the metal trolley beds. "Come on, back on the beds. We can use the element of surprise."

But Paulo was asleep again, sliding down the wall.

The Captain caught him and wriggled him awake. "Come on Paulo." He had to help him back onto his trolley bed, and then he clambered back onto his own. He took one more glance around the room to make sure nothing looked amiss, then he laid down and closed his eyes.

Someone stepped into the room, and the door was closed again. The person moved very slowly and quietly, and soon, the Captain could sense they were standing right beside his bed.

He desperately wanted to see, but dared not

open his eyes. In the next moment though, he found he didn't have to. A voice finally spoke in the quietness of the room.

"Well A7..."

It was A1.

"...Here we are. I'm sorry it's come to this."

The Captain felt him perch himself on the side of the trolley bed.

A1 did a big sigh. "You understand I... I can't keep you anymore. You're just too... dangerous. You and all of your friends."

He heard him shuffle a little in his suit. Moving... Taking something out of his pocket perhaps?

"Everyone out there will think you died from some tragic accident." Then he said in an even more hushed voice, "All my close employees will think that I've sent you to the Underground. And I wish I could, I *really* wish I could."

He shifted again, and the Captain heard a gentle tap, something on glass. Then he felt A1 take a gentle hold of his arm and lift his sleeve to above the elbow.

A needle, thought the Captain. *He has a needle! He's going to...*

The Captain was the next breath away from

scrambling off that bed as far away from that needle as possible, and taking Paulo with him. But a loud alarm suddenly sounded instead. And the needle never came.

An electronic voice blared: INTRUDER ALERT. INTRUDER ALERT.

"What? What intruder?" A1 grumbled. He got up off the trolley. Then the next thing the Captain and Paulo knew, their trolleys were being pushed. Through the lab door and out of the room.

The Captain wanted so much to open his eyes, but he stayed strong and hoped Paulo was as well. In fact, Paulo was probably *actually* just asleep again.

The alarm went on blaring, as A1 blasted through different doors and then into a lift.

He's going back to his office to look at surveillance footage, the Captain realised. *This is good.*

When they burst out of the lift, the Captain could hear A1 mumbling again. "Where are you. *Who* are you?"

Yes... who are they? the Captain wondered.

"Entrance... hallways... nothing, *nothing!*"

Suddenly, the doors to A1's office opened wide.

"The game's up A1!" came a loud voice.

The Captain's eyebrows twitched downwards over his closed eyes.

"What is this?" A1 replied. "A7! How on earth...?!"

The Captain's eyebrows furrowed down even more, and he sneaked a tiny peak, thinking A1 was probably sufficiently distracted. He saw... the side of A1's desk, and Paulo's sleeping head. He would have to make do with listening.

"The name's Ben Cameron," said the loud, elderly voice. "It's always been Ben Cameron, and will always be Ben Cameron."

"As long as you're in the Sanctuary, you're A7," said A1. "And it's obvious we can't have two A7s at once."

He turned back to the Captain and Paulo's beds and the Captain quickly shut his eyes again.

"What is that?" said Ben Cameron. "What are you doing?"

"This is what I should have done to you. And to 7B12, and to D14."

The Captain opened his eyes again. He saw a syringe in A1's hand, right by his head.

"No!" came a new voice. "Stop, stop! Captain? Paulo?"

Evelyn!

"What have you done to them?!" shouted Evie.

Everything in the Captain's body was trying to

make him jump up and tell her they were okay. But he stayed put.

"Looks like we got here just in time," said another girl's voice with an American accent.

"And how, pray, did you get here?" A1 said loudly, over the blaring alarm. He moved away from the trolley beds and around to the front of his desk toward the intruders.

That's all the Captain needed. He silently climbed off the bed, locked eyes with Evie straight away and put a finger to his lips.

Her eye twitched slightly and her lungs gaped in a little gulp of air, but other than that, she did a pretty good job of not giving the Captain away. The others of course had to do the same.

"I had the help of these two young people," said Ben Cameron. "Some lunatic was keeping me in an invisible box in the dark and these two rescued me."

A1 replied, "Well I would expect that from 7B12, but I'm disappointed in you, D14."

The Captain slowly and silently opened some of the drawers in A1's desk, looking for something.

"I thought you were finally starting to settle in," A1 continued. "You even helped me with C36 here..." he almost turned to face Paulo and the Captain.

"Look at me!" Evie yelled, then tried to think of

how to work that into a sentence. "...do... I... *look* like I want to help you?" It was lame, she thought, but it worked. A1's attention was back on her.

"Yes well, obviously there was a little mix up with your appointment time, but then... you disappeared on me!" A1 acted hurt. "You must have wandered far from home."

"I found your little emergency exit." She glanced carefully at the Captain. It looked like he'd found what he was looking for. "And Laura and Mr Cameron are free because of me." When she said it out loud, and realised it was true, she felt empowered. Although, still terrified.

The Captain toggled a couple of switches, wincing at any tiny sound they made.

"And what are you planning to do now?" A1 said. "You've stormed in here with loud, angry voices, but frankly, I don't see the point. Care to fill me in?"

Mr Cameron opened his mouth to speak, but A1 went on. "You realise I can have my loyal employees up here in a matter of seconds to detain you?" He leaned back to his desk to push a button, laying down the syringe for now, and keeping his eyes on the three intruders. "And at my command, they will simply take you back down to the Sanctuary Underground. Except this time, it'll be all three of you. No clever little D14 to come to your rescue." He pushed the same button again, smiling at them.

"Didn't you say you wished you had just... gotten rid of us?" said Mr Cameron, calmly. "Instead of keeping us down there? Why are you about to make the same mistake?"

A1, for the first time, showed the slightest hint of worry in his face. But it wasn't because of what Mr Cameron had just said. He pushed the button again and grumbled, "Come on, come *on*, where are you?"

The Captain realised what the button must have been for. He finally spoke up, sounding as innocent as a child. "Oh, they won't come."

A1 jumped out of his skin and turned to see him, standing over his desk, and all his controls. "A7?!"

"I think you'll find they've grown tired of answering to your beck and call."

"What have you done?"

"It's got something to do with two different buckets, one with special solution in it and one with just water in it, looking very similar. The nurses down there must have got them mixed up."

"The nurses?"

"Alright, *I* got them mixed up, but to be fair, it

is my first day."

Evie pressed her lips together in a smile.

Laura whispered to her, "Who is this guy?"

"Are you alright, Evelyn?" called the Captain.

"Aye aye Captain. I'm all good. What about you?"

"Yes I'm happy as Larry! So's Paulo here." He patted Paulo on the arm. "Aren't you Paulo."

A soft snore sounded from Paulo's throat.

"He's alright," the Captain smiled.

A1 glanced down at the syringe he'd put down on his desk and lunged for it, but the Captain snatched it up first. He held it up and examined it. "Some kind of poison? So you're a murderer, as well as an obsessed, creepy, people-collector?"

"My people here are happy," said A1.

"Are they? Let's see if we can get some evidence on that." The Captain located the buttons he'd found earlier in one of A1's drawers. On the big, curved wall screen, there came a grid of various views of people's loungerooms and living rooms inside the Sanctuary, wherever in their house they had a television. A1 looked up.

On all the televisions in people's houses, was the surveillance view of the Sanctuary Underground that he had stumbled upon earlier.

"What is this?" A1 said, staring up at his big

187

screen. "What's happening? No, no, no. They're not supposed to see that..."

While A1 was distracted, the Captain wriggled Paulo awake again. Paulo wearily sat up and rubbed his eyes. The Captain handed the syringe to him and said quietly, "Here, get rid of this. And go let our friends know we're ready for them."

Paulo stretched and shook himself more awake. Then he slid off his trolley bed and sneaked into the elevator. The Captain hoped he wasn't going to fall back asleep in there.

A1 was still looking at the big screen, distraught. Watching his residents try to make sense of what they were seeing. He lunged back over to his desk to try and undo what the Captain had done.

"It's too late, A1," said the Captain. "They can't unsee it."

Laura turned to Mr Cameron. "Can't we just grab him right now? You know, like a house arrest?"

While her back was turned, A1 grabbed something out of a hidden drawer on his side of the desk, lunged forward towards Laura, holding her tightly and pinning her arms so she couldn't move. "You can try," he said, holding something to her neck. "But if anyone does, 7B12 will die."

"He's bluffing," Laura said. "He's just holding a patch. At best, it'll put me to sleep for a few hours."

"Not for a few hours," the Captain cautioned.

"What?"

"Down in the lab, I saw all the patch solutions. One of them was labelled with a symbol that could mean... that it's a death patch."

"Oooh, I like that name," said A1. "Can I use that?"

"Y-y-you would k-kill me?"

"Oh, 7B12," sighed A1. "What a pity it will be to lose you. I've grown quite fond of you over the years. We've developed quite an interesting relationship, haven't we? Never been a dull moment yet. I was even quite sad to send you to the Sanctuary Underground. Having you here gave me something to do throughout the day. You always kept me on my toes."

"If I could, I'd put you on your *back*. Permanently!"

"Now Laura," said Mr Cameron. "You don't wish to be a killer yourself, do you?"

She tightened her lips, blinked a few times and then confessed, "No."

"May I just... put a word or two in here," said the Captain, getting their attention suddenly. He was still calm. In fact, he'd now seated himself in A1's big swivel chair and had his feet crossed, resting up on the surface of the desk. "The way I see it... is the way everyone will see it."

"What nonsense are you blabbering on about?"

"Well quite literally, the world is watching you. Right from this spot where I sit." He opened his hand towards the little desk-cam which sat on top of A1's desk. He figured A1 used it to do his little personal addresses to the Sanctuary residents from time to time. Now the Captain had it positioned so that it pointed at A1 and Laura.

A1 looked up at his big screen again, and sure enough, he saw himself, live, on everyone's television screen.

"They heard everything, in case you were wondering, and..." the Captain flicked another button and a smaller framed video footage of the front gate of A1's building came up in one corner of the big screen. "Oh look, I found the picture-in-picture mode! And right on cue, there's some people outside. They don't look happy to me. What are you going to do, A1?"

Just then, Paulo arrived with an elevator-full of A1's workers. Covered in muscles, dressed in black, and a patch on their arm that had only been soaked in water. They stomped out and stood with Paulo, glaring at A1 and not looking pleased. To the Captain's surprise, they were all holding something in their hands. Things like metal piping, unscrewed chair or table legs, hammers, wrenches, and other metal tools. And they looked eager to hit something. Or somebody.

"They came up with this bit of the plan on their own, Captain," said Paulo, looking a little more awake.

The Captain looked about to protest, but he stopped himself, and then smiled. "You know, I'm usually not one for solving things with violence. But occasionally," he was gesturing towards A1's controls, "I've been known to make exceptions!"

The workers knew what he meant straight away. They charged forward and started hammering, pounding, beating and smashing all of A1's delicate equipment.

The Captain jumped up from A1's chair, getting well out of the way.

"No!" cried A1. "No, no, no! What are you doing!"

The Captain watched A1 carefully for the moment he took his attention off Laura. When he did, the Captain pulled her away from him and took her, Evie and Mr Cameron to safety near the entrance of the room.

In no time at all, there were sparks flying, bits of equipment chipping up into the air, more alarms going off, and A1's terrible, devastated voice crying out, "No! No! No! No! Stop it! No!!!"

"This is what happens when you give people their free will!" the Captain shouted over all the noise.

"Stop it! Stop it! I order you!" A1 was saying, pulling some of his ex-workers away from the controls. "You're destroying it! You're destroying everything!!"

"That's the general idea," said the Captain, who was leaning his back casually against the wall with his arms folded, watching.

But then, the lift opened again, and more workers dressed in black stormed into the room and stood in a troupe watching the commotion.

"Ha haaa!" A1 shrieked. "Those weren't all of my workers, Captain!"

"I can see that," he replied worriedly, unfolding his arms and lifting his back off the wall.

"*This* troupe's patches won't have expired yet. They've come to my aid!" Then he addressed his patched workers, "Stop these traitors!"

The new troupe rushed in to attack and the unpatched workers were forced to defend themselves. The Captain hustled the others further back outside the door. Paulo came running over to meet them. As both troupes were dressed exactly the same, watching the battle was very confusing and stressful.

Soon, the Captain couldn't even see A1 anymore. The room was a cloud of fighting, struggling, wrestling and tug-of-war. He tried to wade his way through it all to look for him – make sure he wasn't up to anything, but he couldn't find him anywhere. He jumped over a wire flying across the floor and closely escaped a blow on the head with a hammer. He ducked when a circuit board came flying, and skilfully dodged a stumbling ex-worker. Then one bumped into him from behind and thinking he needed to fight him, the worker swung a chair leg at the Captain. It brushed the top of his head before he parried out of the way. It was no use; if he stayed out here in the middle of the battlefield, he was going to get himself severely injured. He returned to where Mr Cameron, Laura and Paulo were crouching, just outside the doorway. Then something immediately struck him.* "Where's Evelyn?" he said.

"We thought she was with you," said Laura.

"She was just here!" The Captain glanced back into the room, trying to see past all the commotion. "I've got to go back in and find her."

"No," said Mr Cameron. "You'll get yourself

---

* Not a chair leg this time, an urgent thought, striking his mind.

severely injured!"

"But Evie could be injured already," said Paulo.

They watched the battle, hoping that the good guys were winning. It was impossible to tell. But on a good note, great things were happening elsewhere as the fighting went on.

Consultants named Sue and Mark were winding down like flat batteries. Surveillance cameras were shutting down all over the Sanctuary.

Then, after a while, the fighting stopped, just like that. The onlookers all stopped breathing for a few seconds.

"Who's won?" asked Mr Cameron.

"I can't tell. They all look the same," said Paulo.

"You were with them when you brought them up," said Laura. "Don't you recognise any of 'em?"

"*That* one I recognise."

"Which guy?"

"...The one on the floor... unconscious."

"That's not good," said Mr Cameron.

But then suddenly, one of the workers left standing looked straight at Paulo and smiled a tired, smile, although not a happy one. They all breathed relief and came back warily into the room.

"We had no idea about what was going on," said one of them. "What A1 was doing..."

"We know," said the Captain. "We know.

Don't worry." He was busy looking for Evie.

"They're all just knocked out," said another.

"Take off their patches," said the Captain, not looking at them, still searching the room. "Tend to their wounds."

"This isn't the end, Captain!" came a bitter voice suddenly.

They all looked for A1, for they knew it was his voice. Smoke and sparks were clouding their view, but soon enough, a new area of A1's office was revealed with the gliding back of part of the wall behind his desk. A1 was standing next to a large glass box, about the same size as the invisible prisons in the Sanctuary Underground. The Captain wondered what it was for, but he was more concerned about what was *inside* the box. Or, to be more precise... *who* was inside.

"Evelyn," he breathed out with dread. *What's he planning*?

"It's all over, A1," said Mr Cameron. "You have to give up now."

"But it's not. I can re-build all this in no time. I did it once, I can do it again. Now if you would all be so kind as to just leave the Sanctuary, I won't harm the former D14."

"What do you mean *just leave*?" said Paulo.

"What do you mean harm her?" said the Captain, taking careful steps toward A1 and the box.

A1 laughed maniacally. "This is a disintegrator, don't you know anything?"

Evie gulped uncontrollably and tears started rolling one after the other down her face.

A1 looked pleased to see the fear in the Captain's eyes.

And then, Evie spoke through her scared, blubbering tears, "You can't just leave, Captain. He'll just patch everyone again and continue this place like nothing's happened. Nothing will have changed. Don't trade all their lives in for mine, you can't do that. I'm just one person."

"Oh do be quiet D14," A1 growled. "Your voice is irritating."

The Captain's shiny blue eyes stared at Evie, speechless. This thirteen-year-old girl had just sacrificed her life for thousands of other people she didn't know. While he was trying to figure out what to say, he saw Laura come into his peripheral vision. Out the corner of his eye, he saw her trying to subtly get his attention.

"Well Captain," shouted A1, "won't you be on your way? I believe the original A7 can show you the way out."

"But you collect people, A1," said the Captain,

trying to look at Laura without actually looking at her. "Why would you let us go?"

"I just want to salvage what I can of this place," A1 said. "And that'll be impossible with you here. I'll just have to make the sacrifice."

The Captain finally glanced at Laura's face, and to his surprise, she was smiling. His brow flickered to a passing frown, but even though he hardly knew Laura, he trusted that smile.

"Oh, how very *big* of you," said the Captain, looking back up at A1. "What a *sacrifice*. After what you heard Evelyn just say, how dare you speak of *your* sacrifice." He glanced down, did a long blink, then looked at Laura, and then back at A1. "But I'm afraid we have no choice. 'No' is my answer to your question. We will not be leaving. Not until we know that you will never again be in control of this so-called Sanctuary. Do what you need to do. We're not giving up."

There was a look of horror on Evie's face as she clasped her hands together and looked up to heaven, before A1 pressed the button on the top of the box. In the blink of an eye, a light came down upon her and zapped her out of existence. "If that's the way you want it. Then so it must be."

"No!!!" cried Mr Cameron immediately, running over towards A1. "You monster! How could you do tha..." His voice faltered. Now face-to-face with A1, he slowly nodded and looked at him as though he was a piece of rotting fruit covered in ants and flies and stinking to high heaven. "Because you're out of your mind. You're a selfish, inhuman, monstrous, maniac!" Mr Cameron, with growing anger, had opened up the glass box, and with his final word 'maniac', he shoved A1 inside.

A1 just chuckled. "Why not? I've not much to live for now." Then he laughed and laughed and laughed until Mr Cameron pressed the 'disintegration' button, and he too was gone.

CHAPTER

WELCOME ABOARD

||||||||||||||||||||||||||||||||||||||||||||||||||

"Well that should get rid of him for a while," said Laura, no longer able to hide her smile.

Mr Cameron's expression changed from sadness and anger to a gaping, confused frown. "For a *while*?"

Laura stuttered, "What? You didn't know?"

"Didn't know what?"

"Captain you seem awfully relaxed as well," said Paulo with a pleading face. "What's going on?"

The Captain merely raised his eyebrows at Laura, looking to her for explanations.

Laura smiled even bigger and said, "Follow me and I'll show you."

As they left the room after Laura, the Captain

said, looking at the casualties in the room, "Er... you'd better er..."

One of the ex-workers finished, "...get them to the Infirmary. Will do!"

"Good, well done," the Captain said hurriedly, and then he was gone. For a change, he was the one at the back of the pack, behind Laura, Paulo and Ben Cameron.

Laura took them all the way back to the organised, lamp-posted forest again. And then down through the dimensional doorway, which the Captain was very fascinated with. "Although, is it meant to be like that, right-angled to each other? If I had a bit of time and my Train, I could fix that."

"It's just down this way a little," said Laura.

"What is?" asked Paulo.

"The Sanctuary Underground," said Mr Cameron, "but why are we..."

"Here!" exclaimed Laura.

They followed her down through the trap door and descended the concrete steps. As soon as they reached the bottom, Laura raced around, looking for something. Some*body*. All the dull lights were still on from when they were down there last.

Although the Captain had seen it on A1's big screen, nothing could have prepared him for the horror and disgrace he felt when he saw it properly.

200

"Here she is!!" they heard Laura calling from a little deeper within the underground expanse. Laura was crouching outside Evie's new little home. Evie's face lit up like sunshine when she saw Laura.

"You scratch my back, I scratch yours, huh!" Laura said with a big smile and released Evie straight away. They hugged. And as soon as Evie saw Paulo, Mr Cameron and the Captain approaching, she hugged each of them as well.

"Thank God you're okay," the Captain said into the top of her head as she hugged him.

"I'm so glad that wasn't a disintegrator," she replied.

The Captain puffed out a big, relieved laugh.

"Who are all these people?" Paulo said gazing wide-eyed into the gloom of the Underground.

"I think they're all ex-residents of the Sanctuary," said the Captain, grimly. "People who, like yourselves, refused to cooperate. Am I right?"

Laura nodded. "Up in the Sanctuary, all these people have 'died'. A1 would make up some story. That's how I came to be down here. He finally trapped me – inescapably this time. Put me in one of those teleport glass box things and I found myself down here. A1 should have realised I'd know he was bluffing when he said it was a disintegrator. What an idiot."

"I think that when you're at the end of your tether, you tend to clutch at anything to try and save yourself. And you make mistakes," said the Captain.

"Well, hadn't we better release all these people?" said Paulo.

"Not until we've found A1," said Mr Cameron. "He must be down here somewhere as well."

They didn't have very far to walk until they came across a curled up, defeated looking A1, huddled in one corner of an invisible box like all the others.

"Ah, there you are," said Mr Cameron. But he wasn't smug. He was sad.

A1's face was blotchy, red, and bitter. The little bit of hair he had was frizzed up and sticking out at odd angles, and he didn't fight to get out or try to say anything. He didn't even look up.

"What do we do with him?" asked Paulo.

"Who, old Geoffrey here?" said Mr Cameron. "I think perhaps, we could leave him down here until he's learnt his lesson. What do you think?"

"And what's going to happen about the Sanctuary?" asked Evie.

"Well, it's a shame to waste that beautiful place up there," said Mr Cameron. "I was thinking of restoring it back to what it was first created for. A holiday resort. I could be the manager, and people can come from all over to have a restful, *temporary* holiday. How does that sound?"

"Sounds great!" said Laura.

"I'll have plenty to keep me busy for a while, fixing everything up. And I'm going to need some help. Perhaps some of A1's employees would like to stay on as my staff. But there'll be no more patches." He then turned to the Captain and his crew. "I don't suppose... would you like to stay on for a bit? A relaxing holiday?"

"I think not," said the Captain. "I think I need a holiday from this place. In fact, I'd like to be on my way."

"Probably for the best. It'll take me a while to get it running properly anyway. And don't worry about these people. I'll get them all out and send them home. All their records will be up in the Infirmary. As for him," Ben Cameron said, referring to A1, "Perhaps after an initial period down here, I'll get him slightly better quarters to stay in. And in a more convenient spot."

"What are you going to do, Laura?" Evie then said, wondering how on earth she was going to thank her for everything she'd done to help. "You don't want to come with us, do you? I'm sure the Captain would welcome you aboard."

"I'd love to, though I don't even know where

you're from, but um..." she started to look up at Mr Cameron. "I was thinking of maybe staying on to help fix this place up, you know sort of, work for Mr Cameron. There's not much for me back home. That is, of course... if he'll have me."

"It's funny," said Ben Cameron. "I was just thinking I'd need an Assistant Manager. Welcome aboard."

Laura beamed. "This is going to be totally cool! Ah, but first, can I just stay for a short holiday? But I want a luxury apartment this time. Not that pokey one I had before."

"Ha ha! Of course! You deserve it young lady!"

"And breakfast in bed every morning!"

"Oh, I'm not sure about that," he said tiredly. "Perhaps one day in the future, the Captain, Evie, and Paulo would like to return. And then *you* can serve the breakfast in bed."

"I'm sure we'd love to visit one day," said the Captain. "Well... *well* in the future. When we've... you know... recovered."

When they did eventually get back to that rocky beach, the Captain and Paulo both shook Mr Cameron's hand heartily. Evie and Laura hugged tightly, and they all said farewell.

"Evelyn," said the Captain as they all stepped up into the carriage room. "What you said earlier astounded me."

"What? Oh. When I was in the glass box? Well, I knew it wasn't *really* a disintegrator, obviously."

The Captain stopped, turned to face her. "No you didn't. I saw your eyes."

"Well I... just thought about all those people. There was nothing else I *could* say. How could I plead for my life when all theirs were at stake?"

"And now there are thousands of people who should be grateful for what you did, but they'll never even know you."

Evie almost got caught up in the thought and felt rather flattered and special. But then she waved a hand, "Na, it was really Laura letting you know he was bluffing that saved the day."

"But you weren't to know that at the time."

"That place kind of degraded the word *sanctuary*, didn't it," Paulo said.

The Captain agreed. "It's frightening what lengths people will go to, to find a bit of rest."

"Well, we all need rest," said Paulo. "Isn't it worth it?"

"Perhaps, but people look in all the wrong places."

Evie smiled to herself, staring at the floor and a soft, thoughtful laugh escaped her.

"Care to share with the rest of us?" said the Captain.

She looked up at the expecting faces of her companions. "Oh, well, that's kind of what I thought when I was hiding in a tree trunk in the dark last night. Something I learnt about sanctuary."

"And what's that?"

"It isn't necessarily a place."

The Captain had started up the Train's engine. It built up steam and he gazed out of one of the cabin windows that looked out onto the beautiful beach; the glistening water, the lush green flora, the whole calm, peaceful, picturesque view, and said, "I shan't be at all sad to leave this place, how about you?"

"Not at all," said Paulo.

"No way!" said Evie. "Let's get out of here!"

"Now, I'm certain that after that experience, you surely couldn't *not* want to go home, Evelyn."

"I didn't even understand that sentence. Too many double negatives. But it sounds like you're trying to get rid of me?"

"I'm not. But remember what I said when you first thought about travelling on the Train?"

"You said it was dangerous."

The Captain was serious for a moment, while he gave Evie some room to make another decision.

"Well," she said eventually, "Obviously I'm missing my family, and obviously I need to return home so they know I'm okay... but..."

"You want another trip."

"Yes please," she replied, hands behind her back, twisting her body from side to side and giving the Captain her sweetest smile. "I need a bit of time to... process everything that's happened before I go home, you know? And anyway it's a time machine, isn't it? I can get back to my parents... well, any *time*... can't I?"

Reluctantly, the Captain said, "Alright. One more trip. But we'll go to the most harmless place I can think of."

"Heaps good!"

"Sounds good to me, too!" said Paulo.

After the Captain set some coordinates, he whirled into action and then the same could be said for the Train. The chugging sound came slowly first, as if it was warming up, and it gradually sped up little by little into that steady rhythmic steam-train sound:

chuff CHOOFETY CHUFF CHOOFETY
chuff CHOOFETY BANG! CHOOFETY
chuff CHOOFETY CHUFF CHOOFETY
chuff CHOOFETY BANG!

It wasn't long until the engine was slowing down again. "Press that button there Evelyn," the Captain said.

"What does it do?"

"It'll materialise us. We'll enter space again."

Evie pressed it and her stomach buzzed with excitement.

"Where are we?" Paulo asked.

"You're free to explore," he told them, pointing towards the door.

They smiled excitedly and crept through the carriage room. Evie reached the carriage room door first. She clutched the handle, took a deep breath and blasted through.

The two of them stumbled out into the open air and found themselves on the footpath of a busy road. Evie's face dropped flat. "Captain!" she complained over her shoulder. "That's not fair!"

The Captain frowned, looking to the carriage door from the engine room. "That's not the reaction I was expecting."

"You look as though you recognise this place," said Paulo.

"I do," Evie pouted. "It's Adelaide. It's Earth. It's home!"

"Pardon?" exclaimed the Captain, and he came tumbling out of the Train too, bumping into the pair of them from behind. "That's odd."

"Don't pretend," said Evie. "I suppose you're right. I should let my parents know I'm okay at least."

"No, honestly," said the Captain. "That wasn't meant to happen! Believe me!" He paused and then frowned as he saw something cross the busy road that they were beside. "...And I don't think *that's* supposed to happen either."

They all looked on. Both Evie and the Captain were utterly bemused, surprised and terrified, all at the same time. Paulo wasn't, because on this planet, he didn't know what was and wasn't normal.

But there it was. Large as life and crossing the road at its own leisure, was a crocodile. A huge, green and gold, scaly, terrifying, real live crocodile.

Paulo was puzzled at their puzzled expressions. "I gather," he said, "that animal doesn't typically wander the streets of Adelaide, then."

Then the crocodile spotted them, opened its mouth in a snarl, and charged...

The Carriage Room

TRAIN MANUAL

Ecclesiastes 3:1-8

There is a time for everything, and a season for every activity under the heavens:

a time to be born and a time to die,
a time to plant and a time to uproot,
a time to kill and a time to heal,
a time to tear down and a time to buil
a time to weep and a time to laugh,
a time to mourn and a time to dance,
a time to scatter stones and a time to
a time to embrace and a time to refra
a time to search and a time to give up
a time to keep and a time to throw a
a time to tear and a time to mend,
a time to be silent and a time to speak,
a time to love and a time to hate,
a time for war and a time for peace.

A false witness will not go unpunished, and whoever pours out lies will perish.

Proverbs 19:9

"Come to me, all of you who are weary and carry heavy burdens, and I will give you REST.

Matt 11:28

You are my hiding place;
you will protect me from trouble
and surround me with songs of deliverance.
Psalm 32:7

It is better to take refuge in the Lord
than to trust in people. Psalm 118:8 (NLT)

✳
dimensions occupying
the same space...?

...Hadn't thought about home
for a long time

I think I'd blocked out some details

Investigate aligning orientation
mismatch between dimensions.

Maybe when we visit in the future,
we can help Ben Cameron with that.

A great holiday destination to keep
in mind ...Hopefully Cameron is still
in charge.

Déjà vu –
French phrase meaning
"already seen"

Common, normal neurological
phenomenon. False memory/
"glitch" in the brain's memory
system

FURRY FRIENDS

There's a monster at school...
...and it's not
...master.

Salt and Light

parasites that defy
earth biology...
            need a human host?

Salt of the Earth...
                came in handy

Ended up in Adelaide
        had to face Evelyn's mother

one of the scariest things I've
                    encountered.

(and I've seen some scary things.)

ABOUT ELIZABETH NEWTON

Elizabeth New ton's perfect Sanctuary home would be a picturesque cottage somewhere quiet with lots of sunlight streaming in and lots of pretty trees around. There would be a room filled with books and a beautiful big desk where she would write all her stories, preferably with a secret entrance and the perfect view outside... with a horse. She would also need a piano in there, and of course, her family close by and a good café down the road. But obviously she would *not* want any surveillance cameras around or anyone trying to hunt her down to stick a patch on her arm.

In reality, she has known the much realer sanctuary that Evie experienced in this story. She knows that inner peace does not come from things made of wood, paper, brick, ivory, horses, or even tea or coffee. Her inner peace comes from Someone else. And it has to, otherwise she'd spend her life chasing fleeting moments of temporary peace... which is so stressful.

In fact, with this inner peace, it's quite possible to find yourself in the middle of a shopping centre, crowded with rushing, crazy people after 80% off sales, at Christmas time, with painful music blaring, babies squalling, toddlers tantruming, sick people coughing near you, sales people asking if you have a minute, out-of-order escalators, *and* people walking too slow in front of you... and still know peace and feel content. Yes. Really.

But this was supposed to be about the author... Elizabeth Newt...
...and we've run out of space.

www.facebook.com/trainflight | trainflightbooks@gmail.com

HAVE ALL THE ADVENTURES!

Season One - Books 1 - 5!

#1 Moon Man

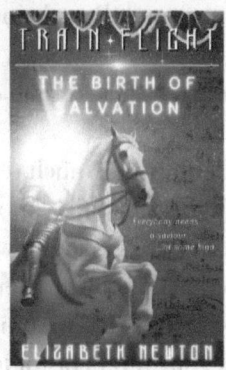

#2 The Birth of Salvation

#3 The Sanctuary

#4 Furry Friends

#5 The End of the Night

Where and When will they go next?

Look out for Season 2!